Lions
An Imprint of HarperCollins*Publishers*

Also available in Lions

The True Confessions of Charlotte Doyle *Avi*
The Mystery of the Cupboard *Lynne Reid Banks*
Children of Winter *Berlie Doherty*
The Moon of Gomrath *Alan Garner*
The Tower Room *Adele Geras*
Children of the Dust *Louise Lawrence*
The Giver *Lois Lowry*
Z for Zachariah *Robert O'Brien*
Class Trip *Bebe Faas Rice*
Deadly Stranger *M. C. Sumner*
The Vandemark Mummy *Cynthia Voigt*

Coming Down To Earth

Lions
An Imprint of HarperCollins*Publishers*

First published in Great Britain in Lions in 1994
1 3 5 7 9 10 8 6 4 2
Lions is an imprint of HarperCollins Children's Books,
a division of HarperCollins Publishers Ltd, 77-85 Fulham
Palace Road, Hammersmith, London W6 8JB

ISBN 0 00 674795 7

Printed and bound in Great Britain
by HarperCollins Manufacturing Ltd, Glasgow

•ONE•

Earth. Earth! Azalin kept watching her feet as they trod over tiles and tarmac. She was standing on, walking on Earth!

She knew, now, what "open air" meant. It was a place where there were no walls and no ceilings. It just went on and on. Miss Ateba had pointed into the air and told them that was "the sky". It went dark and light all by itself; there were no computer-controlled time switches. By day it was blue, and there was a glaring white patch that you couldn't look at – that was the sun. It was ninety million miles away, the guide said, and they could still feel the heat from it.

At night the sky turned black and sparkled with silver stars, which Miss Ateba said were other suns; and up there, somewhere, was their home, Newarth, in its created orbit.

Standing in the damp open air, and looking up into the dark sky made Azalin feel quite dizzy and ill. She almost felt homesick for

Newarth. She was so far away, and there was nothing between her and home but space.

But she was too excited for the homesickness to last more than a second. Whenever she thought about being on Earth, she wanted to dance on the spot and shriek aloud in sheer amazement. Once or twice she had, until Miss Ateba told her to be quiet. Miss Ateba had never liked Azalin much. "Be sporting, Azalin," she said. Azalin pulled a face. She hated that word. She hated being sporting. And, when they went back to Newarth, she would have to spend the rest of her life being sporting.

But never mind Miss Ateba and her sportingness. Azalin had seen the moon shining on water; she'd seen the sun setting and turning the open air to glowing gold, and pink, and deep purple-blue – and it wasn't an effect on a disc-show! This was – the truth was, she didn't know what it was. Miss Ateba and their guide could point and say, "That's the sky; that's the moon; that dazzling glow up there, that's the sun – " The names didn't explain anything. They didn't tell you anything.

Azalin wanted to look at everything, see everything. She stared until her eyes and her head ached. She didn't want to waste time eating. Even the people who went past in the street were worth staring at. It was so strange to see them, really see them, instead of just their images on disc-shows: peculiar people with pale skins that had many colours. Spots of pink, touches of blue, and red noses. Most had hair that was such a pale brown it was almost yellowish. There were crowds of them everywhere – their guide was one of them. Only occasionally did you see a normal-looking person. Their guide was nice in her way, for an Earther, but when she put her face close to Azalin she made Azalin feel queer because her eyes were so pale: a pale grey, as if they were blind.

She seemed to see, but Azalin found it hard to believe that she saw normally, and not in some strange Earth way. Did everything look pale to her? And the guide's flesh was so pale, too, it seemed she might melt if she washed.

In the street they passed one man who had really strange hair. It was purplish, reddish, orangeish – as if his hair had gone rusty! It made them all laugh and point. The guide laughed too, but Miss Ateba was annoyed and hushed them.

"Has he coloured it?" Azalin asked the guide.

"No. Some people have red hair. We say they're quick-tempered!"

Azalin stared after the man as he walked

away down the street, and felt a little shudder of fright. Fancy knowing what someone was going to be like because of their hair!

Too much to see and remember. Even ordinary things, like going to bed, were strange on Earth. She was sharing a room in the hotel with a friend, and the room was huge! It was only for sleeping in, but it was so wastefully big that you could walk into it upright, and there was so much space around the beds that you could walk about! On Newarth there was plenty of space in the Halls, but the private rooms were so small that you had to crawl or slide into them, and once inside there wasn't room to stand up, or to do more than edge up and down the beds.

So much to see, and she'd seen nothing, nothing yet. It was an agony to think that they only had two days before they had to go back to Newarth.

There were places on Earth where trees and flowers grew – well, they grew *in* the Earth. Newarth had lots of trees and flowers – had to have, to keep the oxygen levels high – but even the oldest and biggest of Newarth trees grew in specially made beds, filled with plastic grains impregnated with the necessary chemicals. On Earth trees and flowers grew from the body of the planet itself, as the hairs on Azalin's body grew out of her flesh. When she thought of digging a hole to plant a tree, she was confused by thoughts of digging through into the deck below. It was hard to realise that the Earth was a solid ball of rock and dirt.

Another strange thing about Earth: when you were in the open air, you felt puffs of air against your face. This was the wind, said the guide. The wind wasn't made, either. It just happened. Some winds were so powerful that they could blow buildings down.

"Even buildings like this one?" Azalin asked. They were outside the glass and brick building where they'd eaten lunch. The guide said yes, but those kinds of winds didn't blow in this part of the world. Azalin stared at her. "Well," said the guide, "in some parts of the world it's much hotter than in other parts, and in other parts it's much colder. You get these very strong winds in some parts more often than in others."

Azalin felt as if her brains were fighting inside her skull, fighting to understand, and finding the space too small. "Why do they let the winds blow so strongly?" she asked.

"No one lets the wind blow," the guide reminded her, smiling. "The wind just blows."

"Why?" Azalin asked.

The guide's smile broadened and she raised her hands. "I don't know. It just does. It rains too, you know. Water falls out of the sky."

Azalin tipped back her head to look up at the blue sky. There was no water. "Out of the sky? From up there – out of nothing?"

"I wish it would rain, just for you," said the guide, and then she laughed. "Usually we hope it *won't* rain!"

Azalin frowned as she thought about it. "Does it fall – like out of a tap? Or does it come down like a sprinkler? Or—?"

"Azalin," said Miss Ateba. "Please don't bother the young lady with so many questions."

"Oh, I don't mind her asking questions," the guide said, smiling.

"I do," said Miss Ateba. "Please don't interfere." The guide's face abruptly stopped smiling. Miss Ateba held out her hand. "Azalin, come and walk with me, please." She continued to hold out her hand until Azalin reluctantly took it. To the guide, Miss Ateba said, "Kindly give us your standard talk, and nothing more, if you please." Then she led Azalin away.

It had taken a long, hard campaign to persuade the Education Committee on Newarth to allow Miss Ateba to bring a party of children to Earth. The last thing she wanted was to take back children who had picked up Earth manners. If she did, this would certainly be the last of the trips, and although she would be the first to agree that much about the way of life on Earth was abhorrent, it was so educational for the children to see something of it at first-hand. It would help them understand and appreciate their own society more; it would increase their respect for their ancestors who had left Earth to found Newarth.

"Will it rain before we go?" Azalin asked her teacher. She wanted to see rain very much.

Miss Ateba hesitated. She was a teacher, and she wanted to answer Azalin's question. But she didn't know the answer and, really, she didn't like Earth. It hurt her feelings that Azalin seemed so curious about Earth, and seemed to miss Newarth so little. Miss Ateba missed Newarth. "We shall have to be patient, and wait and see," she said.

"I want it to rain!" Azalin said, looking up in the sky and hanging back, so that she dragged on Miss Ateba's arm.

That annoyed Miss Ateba, who shook Azalin's arm hard. "Behave!" she said. "Stop sulking! Be sporting!" And she dragged Azalin on.

Azalin, who hadn't been sulking, was hurt and angered. I hate you, she thought. And then another thought popped up in her head: I hate Newarth. It took her by surprise, and she lagged behind Miss Ateba as she considered it. She didn't really hate Newarth. It was home; her mother was there, and her father, and Vashti . . .

But I hate it, came the thought again. I don't want to spend my life on Newarth, doing something I hate, day after day after day. With people like Miss Ateba saying, "Be sporting!" when you were unhappy. I can't bear it, she thought. I've got to get out of it. Somehow.

"Azalin!" said Miss Ateba, exasperated by her dragging on her arm again. She hauled Azalin beside her. "Still sulking! Can't you ever be sporting? Can't you?"

Sporting, sporting, sporting! Azalin was no good at being sporting. She couldn't spend her whole life struggling to be sporting, she just couldn't.

Well, then, came the thought. Don't go back to Newarth.

It was a startling thought. Azalin fell quiet and walked beside Miss Ateba as meekly as her teacher could have wished.

She had to go back to Newarth. She had to. Her mother and father were there, and Vashti . . .

But if she went back, she'd have to spend her life as a storekeeper. She felt her muscles bunch with anger at the prospect; she seemed to swell with frustration and despair. She couldn't. Not her whole life, not every day of every week and month and year . . .

So, don't go back to Newarth.

She would have to make up her mind soon – their time on Earth was quickly running out. They had one more night in the huge bedroom at the hotel and then, the next morning, they would board the shuttle again, and fly home.

They were on their way back to the hotel after having been on a little outing to collect presents to take home with them: little boxes of biscuits and chocolates, with pictures of the planet Earth on the box. As they neared the hotel, they passed a coach. People crowded around its door, eager to get on. There was a pile of luggage, waiting to be loaded. The luggage compartments stood open.

Azalin was walking at the back of her group, a little way behind them. She saw the coach, the people, the open compartment. No one was looking at her. And the open luggage compartment was so tempting, just the right height for her to roll inside. She hung back a little further. No one from her own party looked back.

She watched as the people climbed on to the coach. She drew close to the side of the vehicle herself, partly hiding herself behind it.

The last of the people went up the steps and the driver, instead of coming to load the bags, got on to the coach too. No one could see her. If she kept close to the side of the coach, not even the people on board it would be able to see her. She darted forward and rolled herself into the luggage compartment.

The floor was hard, cool and metallic beneath her hands and knees, but gritty with dust. She crawled forward, further in, and saw that some bags had already been loaded: some suitcases, and some soft bags that formed large rolls. Hurriedly, she dragged a soft bag against the hard wall of the coach, and leaned on it. Then she dragged a suitcase into place, to hide herself from the coach driver, when he came to load the other bags. It was awkward, and heavy, and she could only drag it from a kneeling position. But she got it into place and lay huddled behind it, her knees and feet drawn up, hoping that she wouldn't be noticed, hoping that the coach driver wouldn't notice that the bags had been moved.

He didn't. He heaved heavy bags into the compartment and shoved them to the back. The metal floor under Azalin trembled. The bags landed with crashing thumps, and the driver banged and shoved the cases into the side of the coach, and threw them on top of one another. It was almost as if he was trying to hurt her, although he didn't even know she was there. A bag, thrown on top of a case, toppled down on her, and she gasped before she realised that it hadn't hurt her: it was a soft bag, packed fat with clothes. It landed on her heavily, but softly.

And then, after a furious, frightening few minutes of bangs and bounces, all the luggage was loaded, and the driver closed the compartment. Azalin was closed in darkness. She lay still, listening. From above her came quiet bumps and stirrings, and what might have been voices; from outside came sharper, louder sounds of passing traffic. Was it too late, she suddenly wondered, to get out of there? To hammer on the doors and shout to be let out?

A vibrating shudder ran through the coach, shaking Azalin's very bones, shaking her teeth. The engine had been started. With a jolt that threw her backwards, and set all the cases lurching towards her, the coach drew away.

•TWO•

Just three weeks before they had left Newarth for Earth, it had been Azalin's eleventh birthday. A birthday party had been held for her in the canteen of her Hall of Residence – for her and a couple of other children who'd been born on the same day. The Halls had birthday parties for all of their residents, and every other resident was expected to attend. If anyone was absent, unless they had a very good excuse, people said they were unsporting.

Azalin and the other birthday children had been given a present by every other resident in their Hall. Some of the presents were very small – a flower, a little box of sweets – while some of the younger children offered bits of chewed ribbon or broken toys. It wasn't the present that was important; it was the fact that a present had been given. If someone was a member of your Hall, they were a member of your family, and you showed it by attending their party and giving them something – it was shocking bad manners not to do either. Being at the party and giving a present was all part of being sporting.

If you were the person the party was for, you had to thank everyone for being there, and for their present, and the smaller the present, the more you thanked them. That was part of being sporting too. But try as hard as she could, Azalin couldn't feel very grateful for a doll with one arm missing, and flowers didn't make her very thankful either.

She felt ashamed as she said thank you, because she didn't really feel grateful, but she didn't know how she could make herself feel grateful when she wasn't. That was why she hated being sporting. It was all about pretending and lying, and she just wasn't very good at it.

So she had looked forward to the presents from her mother and father, and from her mother's sister, Vashti. They would be the best. Vashti had already given her one present, a secret one. Vashti was great. She was a 'tronic, and she knew everything about electronics and she could fix anything. That made her a very important person on Newarth, where so many of the systems depended on electronics. Of course, no one was supposed to be more important than anyone else, but that was more sportingness. If the truth was told, electronics on Newarth controlled the lights that made their "day" and "night"; it controlled the heating, not only for the people and animals, but for the plants in the greenhouses on the farm and recreation levels. It controlled the creation, recycling and purifying of water; it monitored the levels of water in the air; and also the content of the air, to ensure that there was enough oxygen for the people, and enough carbon dioxide for the plants and microbes. And there were hundreds – probably thousands – of less vital uses for electronics as well: telephones, ovens and fridges in the canteens, disc-shows and computer games for entertainment, the lifts between levels . . .

There were miles and miles and miles of electric cable running through all the levels of Newarth; there were millions of circuit boards, countless chips. And Vashti, her Vashti, was one of the great army of people who constantly repaired and maintained this electronic network, and kept Newarth alive. It made Azalin's heart swell and grow warm to think of it. It was romantic; it was wonderful. She was going to be a 'tronic, like Vashti. Everyone on Newarth, at around the age of eleven or twelve, was apprenticed to the trade they would follow for the rest of their lives.

Both Vashti and Deborah had promised to ask if Azalin's apprenticeship could be in electronics.

About a fortnight before her birthday, Azalin had been in her Hall of Residence, playing a computer game with a friend, when Vashti had appeared and said, "Come with me."

"You win," Azalin had said to her friend, giving up the game, because it was usually worth going with Vashti.

The Halls were big, and high, and one wall was lined with tier after tier of private cells, with steps and landings leading to them. Some, like the one Vashti lived in, were only big enough for one person. Others, like the one Azalin shared with her mother, were big enough for two. Vashti led the way to her own cell, and they'd both squeezed into it, and sat side by side on the narrow bed. Vashti had opened one of the drawers that were fitted into the base of the bed and had lifted out, by its leg, a crab, which she dropped into Azalin's lap. "There," she said. "Part of your present. Don't tell anybody."

Azalin lifted up the crab and clacked its plastic legs delightedly. The crabs crawled everywhere, all over Newarth. There were special holes in the ceilings of every cell, for them to crawl in and out. They clacked about the ceilings of the corridors, and through all the levels, and most people were so used to seeing them that they took no notice of them at all. Azalin loved them.

They were maintenance robots. It was their job to follow and monitor the miles of electrical cable – they even crawled about Newarth's outer skin, in space. Whenever they detected a fault, they sent back a signal to a central computer. If the fault was a very simple one, the computer gave them permission to repair it themselves – otherwise the computer alerted a maintenance crew.

"How did you get it?" Azalin asked.

"It's a reject," Vashti said. "It keeps signalling faults where there aren't any. It was just going to be junked, but I thought: I know someone who'd like that."

"I thought you might like to try finding out what's wrong with it."

Azalin frowned. If real 'tronics couldn't fix the crab, how could she?

"It's a simple fault," Vashti said. "It's just not worth our time fixing it. Cheaper to make a new crab. But your time ain't money. Have a go at isolating the fault – and I'll tell you if you've got it right."

Azalin had picked up a lot about electronics, with Vashti's help, from reading the books in Newarth's library. There were disc-books and a few of the old, paper kind.

She'd been surprised by how easy isolating the fault was – so easy that she suspected she was wrong. But Vashti said no, well done, right first time. "You're almost as good a 'tronic as me already," Vashti had said, which had made Azalin so happy, she wanted to pop like popcorn. So that was *one* present Vashti had already given her. But she knew she had another, because Vashti had said so. And then there would be presents from her mother and father too.

Her father, and the fathers of the other birthday children, had come along to the Hall as guests. Azalin's father came to see her every day, and she was especially proud of him at the birthday party, because he looked so handsome. He was tall and thin, dressed all in black, with a short, curly black beard and a big smile. When it came to his turn in the present-giving, he kissed Azalin, gave her a red rose, and then said loudly, so everyone could hear, "We have two invisible presents. Here's the first one: your mother and I have decided that you can go on the trip to Earth."

The people gathered around her clapped and cheered. To do otherwise would have been unsporting. But not all of the applause was as enthusiastic as it might have been. Not everyone approved of the trip to Earth.

Deborah, Azalin's mother, must have sensed the hidden disapproval, because she said, "All of us came from Earth once."

"Yes," someone said, "but we had the sense to leave it." And there was laughter, to show that it wasn't meant unkindly.

"All you Earth trippers, mind you don't pick up bad influences," said someone else, in a joking tone.

"We are only going for three days," Miss Ateba said.

"They'll hardly have time to look round the space-port before they have to come back," said Vashti. Deborah fidgeted. She hadn't really wanted Azalin to go, but Hassan and Vashti had talked her into it.

Hassan had been eager to change the subject. "Let's give you—"

"Wait," Vashti said. "You've given her one present, and mine isn't invisible. Let me give her mine first." And Vashti had handed Azalin a video-disc all about Earth. "So you can see the bits you won't have time to see when you're there."

"Now our other invisible present," Deborah said, as Azalin kissed Vashti. "Azalin, we've got you an apprenticeship."

Azalin froze, her mouth open. From all around there came loud, enthusiastic applause and cheers. Becoming apprenticed was as big an event as being born, or having your own child: it marked a person's becoming a useful member of Newarth. No more lessons from Miss Ateba! Azalin thought. She was almost grown up. People wouldn't be able to order her about so much any more.

"You start as soon as you're twelve," Hassan said.

Another year with Miss Ateba, then. But never mind, only a year. Azalin made up a dance on the spot, spinning round and tapping her feet. The people gathered round clapped again, and laughed.

"You're going to be like me," Hassan said. "You're going to be a storekeeper."

The words were like a cuff around the ear. Azalin stopped dancing and stared at him. She hoped that she'd misheard. "A what?"

"It's an important job, storekeeper," Hassan had said quickly. "The whole of Newarth would come to a stop without us storekeepers."

That was true. Newarth needed constant repair, and that meant that there must always be ready supplies of nuts, bolts, rivets, clips, drums of wire, resisters, chips, insulation, spanners, wire cutters and many, many other things, such as welding torches, gas canisters, face masks. Someone had to do the job of keeping count of all these things, of how many had been used, how many were left. Someone had to make sure that fresh stocks were ordered well before old stocks ran out, and that Newarth's factories were requested to manufacture the new components. It was a vital job. Newarth would die without it.

That was what the storekeepers said anyway, but it was only partly true. In fact, almost all the work was done by computers. The storekeepers were really only there to mind the computer, and pack things away in the storerooms and fetch them out again. Very occasionally, they had to take over the whole job when the computer went down, and they had to be trained to do it, but they very rarely had to. Yes, storekeeping was an important job – but one of the most boring that anyone could do.

"But I want to be a 'tronic," Azalin had said. It always helped in getting an apprenticeship if you had family in the same line of work, and with Vashti being a 'tronic, and her mother working in programming, Azalin had thought she would get a 'tronic 'prenticeship easily. Her parents had reminded her that it wasn't up to them, though they would do their best, and that she should remember that there might not be any 'tronic places available, but Azalin hadn't really listened.

"We tried our best," Deborah said. "Didn't we, Vashti?"

Vashti nodded. "Did everything we could. But there aren't any places for 'tronics – won't be for two or three years."

Hassan had given his big smile, and had crouched down to put his arms around his daughter. "I know you're a little bit disappointed, but cheer up! You just throw yourself into your training and—"

"I don't want to be a storekeeper!" Azalin had shouted, and had wrenched herself out of her father's arms. "I don't want to mind computers! I want to fix them!"

Many people had begun leaving the canteen, taking children with them. They didn't want their children to see Azalin behaving so unsportingly.

There had been a terrible row, with her mother threatening not to let her go to Earth after all, and her father saying that would be unsporting, and that they had to set an example of sportingness to Azalin. "Listen, my girl," he'd said to Azalin. "You're almost grown-up and grown-up people are sporting. Whatever job they're given, they do that job as well as they can. I didn't choose to be a storekeeper, but I enjoy the job and I'm good at it. Your mother didn't choose to be in software; Vashti didn't choose to be a 'tronic. But we're all good at our jobs. We don't have enough people on Newarth for everyone to be able to do the job they'd most like. What would happen if everyone started saying, 'I won't do this job, I don't like it'?"

What a liar, Azalin thought. How could anyone enjoy being a storekeeper?

"Why can't I wait until there's a 'tronic place?" she'd said.

"Azalin!" Her mother was always quick to lose her temper. "No one waits until they're fourteen or fifteen for an apprenticeship!"

It was true, no one did. So she couldn't. It would, of course, be unsporting, and rather than be unsporting, it would be better for her to spend her whole life sitting in front of a computer, or fetching things out of a storeroom. Years and years of boredom. Her whole life wasted. It would be better to be dead.

"You'll be a storekeeper," her mother had said, "and you'll be a good one, and you'll thank your father for getting you the apprenticeship!"

That was being sporting.

But Azalin didn't want to be a storekeeper. "Leave her alone," people said. "She'll get used to it." Hearing that made Azalin all the more determined not to get used to it. In bed at night she said to herself, "I am not going to be a storekeeper!"

In the cold, jolting, roaring dark of the coach's luggage compartment, as the coach hurtled towards she didn't know where, she comforted herself with the thought that at least she wasn't going to be a storekeeper. Almost anything else might happen to her, but not that.

"See?" She sent her thoughts through millions of miles to her parents on Newarth. "You can't make me do anything!"

And then, when she was shaking with cold, and bruised with the coach's bumps, and deaf from its noise – it stopped.

•THREE•

The passengers clambered stiffly from the coach, and stood waiting as the driver opened the luggage compartments on either side of the vehicle. The people waiting on one side were startled by a case suddenly jumping from the compartment and landing with a thud on the tarmac. The driver was busy on the other side of the coach.

Out of the compartment itself, a small, dirty girl came rolling. She landed in a deep crouch, and a soft bag fell out after her. Then she was on her feet and, dodging between the passengers, ran away across the car park.

People stood staring after her, though she soon disappeared among the parked cars and coaches. They turned to each other. "A girl!" they said. "In with the luggage!"

Someone hurried around the coach to tell the driver. He didn't believe them. "I loaded the bags," he said. "There was nobody in there." Other people began to insist that they, too, had seen the little girl. But by then, Azalin was well away.

She had run from the car park to a place of trees and flowerbeds and large buildings surrounded by lawns. People were wheeling piles of baggage on trolleys up to the doors. Either they were all coming home at the same time, or they didn't live here . . . Of course, these buildings were hotels, like the one she'd stayed in with Miss Ateba. She remembered their guide talking about the "superb tourist facilities" and the so-many thousands of visitors her city recieved every year. The coach must have brought her to another city where people went to look at buildings and statues and rivers and rain. Azalin herself kept looking at the trees and the way their branches moved against the open air.

The lawns and hotels led into the streets of the city. Every building was a different shape, and some were very strange. And there was a fountain where the spouting water was enclosed within a cage made of whirling birds. The birds were metal, but they moved, and sparkled in the light and the water. It was pretty. She wasn't the only person looking at it. A boy beside her spoke. "It's good here, isn't it?" he said.

Azalin wasn't sure, at first, that he was speaking to her. When she saw that he was, she nodded, but couldn't stop herself from edging a couple of steps away from him.

"I'm having a last look round," the boy said. "We're leaving tomorrow. When are you leaving?"

Feeling shy, she muttered, "Don't know." She felt uneasy at suddenly finding herself talking to a wild Earther, and not a tame one, like the guide. Would he attack her? she wondered. Earthers attacked each other all the time: it was one of the reasons why Newarth had been reluctant to allow Miss Ateba to bring them to Earth.

"We've been here a week," said the boy. "Have you seen the castle yet?"

Azalin edged further away. The boy might only be talking to her to catch her off guard before he hit her and tried to take her belongings. She lost her nerve and walked quickly away from him.

But there were Earthers all around her as she walked on along the street. They walked in twos and in larger groups: men with women, women with children, men and women with children. Most of them were laughing or smiling, and they didn't seem dangerous.

There was a frilly sort of building, all red and gold. A notice outside said it was a "pagoda". Inside it was a restaurant, and

Azalin went in and helped herself to food from the serving hatches. Earthers queued behind her, and didn't try to push her out of the way. No one tried to rob her of her food as she carried it to an empty table. She looked around, watching them, as she ate her hamburger, and no one seemed to be taking much notice of her. She relaxed a little and, as she drank her milkshake, began to think about what she was going to do now that she'd got away from Miss Ateba. She wouldn't be going back to Newarth just yet; but sooner or later she would have to go. But not as a storekeeper.

As she walked up the street from the fountain, she'd seen a block of telephones. Now she left the restaurant and went back to the phones. There was, as she'd hoped, a notice above the phones, explaining how you used them, and she put her hands behind her back and carefully read it. There was a section on making "Off-Earth Calls" and another on "Asking for the Operator." It seemed easier than she'd thought it might be.

She picked up the phone and dialled for the operator. "I'd like to make a reversed charges call, please."

"What town?"

"An Off-Earth call, please. I'd like to call Newarth, please."

"Certainly. Who do you wish to call on Newarth?"

Azalin hesitated. She had intended to ask to speak to her mother, but her mother would be sure to be annoyed by what she had to say. "Could I just leave a message?"

"Certainly. Who do you wish to leave the message for?"

"Oh. For Deborah Rupkina. She lives in Hall 504, on Newarth."

"Recording you now," said the operator. "Speak after the tone."

Azalin waited through a few seconds of silence, and then for the bleep of the tone. Then she gabbled, "Mum? Mum, this is Azalin. I'm on Earth. I've run away from Miss Ateba and I'm not coming back – not until you let me be a 'tronic anyway. Er . . . I'll phone again. When I can be a 'tronic I'll come back, but not until then."

She slammed the phone back on its cradle, and ran away down the street. There was another fountain and she ran around it, and jumped up on to its low wall and danced on it, being splashed by the wind-blown water. She felt pleased with herself. They would have to let her be a 'tronic now. When the message was played back, and they realised that she was all alone on Earth, where people were murdered every day, they'd have to let her be a 'tronic, just to get her back.

She realised that some of the Earthers were watching her as she danced around the fountain's edge, and were laughing at her.

"You'll fall in!" one shouted.

She jumped down and ran away from the fountain until she was lost in the crowds of Earthers. Out of breath, she sat down on a bench that was hung about with flowers and watched the people go by. In this city there didn't seem to be any of the big noisy vehicles that had always been juddering by in the city where she'd been with Miss Ateba. Here there were just people, walking about, looking at things, and laughing. It seemed a much nicer place. Azalin wondered why they hadn't come here in the first place. How many of these people were murderers? She supposed that she should be frightened, being here all alone but, in the sunshine of this happy place, she didn't. She felt brave, and clever and strong.

They'll play back my message, she thought, and then another thought occurred to her. Her mother and the others on Newarth wouldn't give in immediately. First they'd try to get her back. They'd have the call traced. Azalin knew enough about electronics to know that this wouldn't be difficult. A very short while after the call had been played back, Newarth would know where she'd made the call from, and they'd send people here – wherever she was – and they'd search for her. Or they'd get the Earthers to do it for them.

I have to stay out of sight, she thought; and she was angry with herself for dancing on the fountain, and drawing attention to herself.

And when I phone back, she thought, I must do it from a different place.

But in the meantime, she might as well have a look around this place and see what there was to see.

There was too much to see, and she got tired and hungry as she tramped about on sore feet. Crowds of people everywhere, stopping to watch jugglers and tight-rope walkers. White buildings shaped like balls cut in half; buildings made from tree trunks; buildings seemingly made all of glass, tall thin buildings, and a building shaped like a can of drink. She went for a ride on a boat, and then had something to eat in a restaurant made all of wood, and where the waitresses wore their hair in plaits, and hats with horns sticking out of the side. And still the streets were full of crowds of people, walking about, going in and out of the buildings, sitting on the benches, and all wearing bright clothes. Azalin realised what had been bothering her. Why were none of them wearing overalls for work? In fact, no one seemed to work in this Earth city. In the city where she'd stayed with Miss Ateba there had been the people at the hotel, who wore overalls or uniforms ... there had been the guide ... And you could spot the workers in the street. They wore darker, heavier clothes, and they weren't just wandering. You could tell they were going somewhere, to do something.

Perhaps some people on Earth didn't work? She'd heard that said on Newarth. "On Earth they have too many people and not enough jobs," they said. She should be lucky, she'd been told, that she was going to get a job as a storekeeper. It might not be the job she wanted to do, but at least she would have a job, and would know that she was useful. Were all these Earthers around her the useless ones who had no jobs? If so, they seemed to be having a good time. Why couldn't Newarth be like this? Let people who wanted to be storekeepers be storekeepers – but, if you couldn't do the job you wanted to do, why couldn't you come to a place like this and be happy instead of being bored? Things were managed much better on Earth, Azalin thought, than they were on Newarth.

She wandered into some narrow streets, where the pavement under her feet was made of rounded stones. It was quite difficult to walk on. The houses all had small windows and doors, and some of them had walls which were out of true. It was getting later now, and the light was beginning to fade. On Newarth light faded and brightened with day and night but, on Newarth, it was controlled by computer time switches. Azalin kept staring up into the open air of Earth, and wondering what told the light to fade here. She'd been told about the sun, and the Earth turning on its axis, but that didn't explain much – what told the sun to move and the Earth to spin?

But, as it grew darker, Azalin began to feel less happy. She couldn't help noticing that there were fewer and fewer children of her own age in the streets, which made her more noticeable. The growing dark made her nervous too. It was harder to feel brave than it had been in the bright sunshine. She kept remembering things she had heard on Newarth about how many murders were committed on Earth. She came upon a building with open doors, which was brightly lit. There was a small group of people inside, and they were laughing, which made Azalin feel she would be safer inside with them. Murderers probably weren't people who laughed much. The doors of the place stood open, so she went in.

The group of people walked ahead of her and disappeared through a pair of double doors. Azalin followed them over the thick red carpet, and hesitated at the door. But, from behind it, she heard music and applause.

The door was heavy and she had to lean on it hard before it opened, admitting her into darkness. She blundered forward and bumped into a wall, along which she had to grope her way. From ahead of her, from the other side of the wall, came the sigh and rustle of crowds of people, and music; and she was surrounded by a smell of carpets, and perfume and polish.

Then she came, suddenly, to a gap in the wall and saw, at a distance, a brightly lit stage. In the dark below the stage were the dim shapes of seated people, all looking towards the bright light.

Alone on the stage stood a slight, doll-like figure, dressed all in black, except for his brilliantly white shirt and white gloves. As Azalin watched, the figure took a tall black hat from its head with a graceful, bowing motion and tilted it towards the audience so that everyone could see inside. There was nothing in the hat. With another graceful movement, the black-dressed figure up-ended the hat and, from inside it, fell flowers, bright red and white flowers. They poured from the hat and made a mound on the stage. And yet the hat had been empty!

It was so pretty to watch that Azalin couldn't help smiling with pleasure. And still the flowers were pouring from the hat, more and more of them. The man on the stage moved around, to make room for them all, until he was ankle-deep in red and white flowers wherever he moved. As more and more flowers poured out, the people in the audience began to laugh, and children could be heard squealing. Azalin began to laugh too. She couldn't help it.

When the stage was completely covered, and the flowers were mounded up in places, the man put the hat on his head again, with another graceful bow. The audience clapped and clapped, and Azalin joined in. In the middle of all the noise, she saw an empty seat in front of her, a few steps down, and hurried to slide into it.

The man on the stage went on to dance with his walking cane, which floated in the air, bowing to him, and turning with him. Then he threw the cane into the air, and it disappeared, just vanished. Then he drove a sword through himself – the point of the sword could be seen sticking out of his back – grinned at the audience and pulled the sword out again. And then he disappeared. He was standing right in the middle of the stage, brightly lit, and then – the stage was empty. The applause was very loud.

But the next on to the stage was a woman in a long dress who sang three songs, each more boring than the one before. And Azalin, after walking about all day, began to feel very sleepy in the warmth and half-darkness. Every time she began to fall asleep, a burst of applause would wake her with a shock. She had to go somewhere else, she decided: somewhere quiet and out of the way where she could sleep.

She slipped out of her seat, and went quickly down an aisle, and pushed open another heavy door. It wasn't the same door that she'd come in by. She found herself in a dim and rather drab corridor with bare floorboards. The heavy door swung shut behind her, and the sound of music and applause dropped to a whisper. She went along the corridor, turned a corner, went through another door, and found herself in another stretch of drab corridor, with many closed doors. It wasn't as easy to find her way out as it had been to find her way in. But then, she was looking for somewhere to sleep, and there was probably somewhere in here that she could bed down.

She put her ear to one of the closed doors.

No sound came from inside. Carefully, she eased the door open. No sound of surprise or movement came from inside, and she shoved the door right open.

The room was suddenly lit by a brilliant light, and a voice said, "A typical dressing room. Here you see the star's make-up on her table, the flowers from an admirer, the cards from wellwishers . . ." Azalin jumped with fright, and then froze, though her heart went on leaping and skipping – but then realised that there was no one else in the room. The light and the recording had been switched on by her opening the door. Ignoring the voice, she went into the room and closed the door behind her.

There was a dressing table with a big mirror, and a lamp that was supposed to be a gas lamp but which was really electric. The surface of the dressing table was covered with powder, and sticks of make-up. A huge bunch of flowers stood in a vase on a table to one side. Cards were stuck all round the mirror. But what took Azalin's eye was the chaise longue.

Gratefully, she sat down on it. The room was obviously a place that people were meant to come and look at, so it wasn't a very good place to go to sleep, but she couldn't resist lying down, just for a few minutes. She could still hear, very faintly, the sound of music, so the show was still going on. No one would come for a while. She'd go before then, after she'd had a little rest.

She lay down. A couple of minutes later the light switched itself off. She hardly noticed.

When she woke it was dark, cold, and very, very quiet. She sat up and knew that she was alone in the middle of the night. She listened, but there was no sound. The show was long over.

It was the cold that had woken her. Her whole body was chilled. She got up and groped about in the dark, feeling for the door she'd come in by. When she found it, and opened it, the light snapped on, dazzling her, and a voice said, "A typical dressing room– "

Azalin collapsed against the door jamb, her heart thumping. She'd forgotten all about the break-circuit door. In such quiet, the voice seemed to bellow. She slipped out into the corridor, letting the door shut behind her. The light went out as the door clicked closed, and the voice stopped.

She was confused in the dark, and didn't know whether she was heading for the door to the outside, or going further into the building. There was no sound of music to guide her. Walking slowly and carefully down the middle of the corridor, she turned round to consider which way she ought to go, and backed, with a thump, into someone who was standing quietly in the dark.

•FOUR•

Deborah Rupkina slowly climbed the staircase to her landing, looking forward to her bed, but feeling a little sad that, tonight, she would be sleeping in her cell alone. All day, as she worked, her thoughts had kept returning to Azalin. Even the evening, spent in the Hall's bar with Vashti and some friends, hadn't stopped her thinking of Azalin.

"She's enjoying herself and hasn't given you a thought," Vashti had said.

Deborah hoped so. She wanted Azalin to enjoy her time on Earth, and not be homesick. There were worse things than homesickness, of course. Earth was a dangerous place. But Miss Ateba was there to look after them, and Gosia Ateba was a sensible, capable woman. She wouldn't take any risks.

Deborah came to the door of her cell and set her hand against the panel. The door slid back. She was too tired to grasp the hand, grip above the door and swing herself in feet first.

Instead she crawled in, head first, and then clambered up to sit on the bed before touching the button that closed the door.

The cell was tiny, long enough for Deborah to stretch out at full length, but not high enough for her to stand up. A bed ran the length of each wall, with storage space beneath them, and a narrow aisle between them. A television screen occupied most of the end wall, with a shelf below it for the audio/video machine, and its discs.

Deborah lay on the bed, and was about to choose a channel on the television, when she noticed that a red light was showing on the wall-mounted phone. There was a message for her. Azalin, she thought immediately, and reached up for the receiver.

She tapped in the number that would authorise the Hall's computer to release her message. Fancy Azalin being thoughtful enough to ring me, she thought. She's more grown up than I thought. Smiling, feeling fond of her daughter, she held the receiver to her ear and waited for the message to come through.

"MUM? MUM, THIS IS AZALIN. I'M ON EARTH. I'VE RUN AWAY FROM MISS ATEBA AND I'M NOT COMING BACK – NOT UNTIL YOU LET ME BE A 'TRONIC

ANYWAY. ER – I'LL PHONE AGAIN. WHEN I CAN BE A 'TRONIC I'LL COME BACK, BUT NOT UNTIL THEN."

End of message.

Deborah sat on her bed, the phone still in her hand. Then she tapped in the order Replay Tape, and listened to her daughter's voice all over again. When the message once more came to an end, she threw the receiver on the bed, with tears in her eyes, and shouted, "Oh Azalin!"

Her fists clenched with anger; she punched the wall. "Azalin! You– !"

What to do? What could she do? She would have liked to have given Azalin a good hiding – but Azalin was a few million miles out of reach. In the midst of her anger, Deborah's heart seemed to squeeze small and cold as she realised that Azalin was on Earth, and out of reach, and alone.

"Oh no," she said aloud, and turned towards the door – and then thought the phone would be quicker, and picked up the receiver – and then stopped as she thought what she would have to say: "My daughter has run away from her teacher. She's trying to blackmail Newarth. She's being unsporting." She found herself trembling at the mere idea of saying it. How people would look at her;

how they would frown and pull their mouths down. Everyone would think what a bad mother she was, to raise such an unsporting daughter. In eleven years, hadn't she taught Azalin any values? Years and years from now people would point her out and say, "You see that woman. She's the mother of Azalin who–" And Azalin herself would never be forgiven. Always it would be remembered and held against her, that she had been so unsporting, so troublesome.

I must keep it secret, Deborah thought. For Azalin's sake, to give her a chance for her future. Say nothing. Miss Ateba will find that Azalin's missing very soon – probably already has. Let her carry the can for losing her. She should have kept a better eye on her anyway. And all Deborah's anger rose up again, but directed at Miss Ateba now. What had the woman been playing at, to let Azalin get away from her? How dare she be so careless with other people's children.

Other people's children — she would have to tell Hassan that his daughter was missing, wouldn't she? Perhaps he would know what to do . . . But no. He would blame her too, he would say that she hadn't set Azalin a good enough example of sportingness. Well, let him find out when Miss Ateba took the blame.

But Azalin was alone on Earth. Deborah clutched at her face with both hands, feeling the flesh grow hard as the blood drained from it, and wondered how she could ever have thought of keeping what Azalin had done secret. She had to go to the authorities, she had to tell someone and get help, get a search started. Her heart began to beat fast as she thought of it, both in fear for Azalin and fear of her own shame.

Gina! She had to find Gina, the Hall Rep. Gina would know what to do, who to report to. Deborah turned to the door again, and opened it with a touch. Grasping the hand-grip above the door, she swung her feet out on to the walkway, all tiredness forgotten. Azalin, all alone on Earth, would find trouble, nothing was more certain. She must be frightened by now, she might be hungry, cold – and who might she have met?

Deborah ran along the walkway to the steps and began running down. Half leaning over the rail as she went, she yelled at the people below, "Gina! Where's Gina?" Startled faces lifted to her.

She reached the bottom of the stairs and strode across the floor towards the few people still seated in the soft chairs of the bar. And, before she could shout for her again, there was Gina coming towards her, a Gina who looked anxious and almost afraid, as if she already knew . . .

"Deborah," Gina said, holding out both hands. "Come and sit down. I've got bad news."

Azalin's dead, Deborah thought immediately. She was too afraid, and too hopeful of being wrong, to have anything to say. She went with Gina to the bar, and someone stood up to let her have a seat. She looked at Gina, fixed her eyes on her.

Gina crouched down in front of Deborah and said, "We've had a phone call from Gosia Ateba on the shuttle . . ." Gina looked away, licked her lips, before looking directly at Deborah with wide eyes. "Azalin won't be coming back with the others, I'm afraid. She's missing."

Deborah said nothing. The people around her mistook her silence for shock. Deborah was thinking: now they know. I don't have to say anything. I can let them think it was all Miss Ateba's fault.

"It seems," Gina said, "that they went back to the place where they were staying the night before they started home, and Gosia counted up the children, and Azalin wasn't with them."

"Well, where is she?" Deborah demanded. "Didn't she look for her?"

Gina touched Deborah's arm. "Of course she looked for her. They searched high and low, for hours. They just couldn't find her . . . They know she was with them not long before they got to the hotel, because one of the other children remembers talking to her . . . So she can't be far. There are people on Earth still looking for her. They'll soon find her – and then they'll send her home on the first shuttle. It'll be all right, you'll see."

"But what's happened to her?" Deborah shouted. "What do you mean, she's gone missing? Azalin wouldn't go off by herself, would she?"

"We don't know what's happened yet," Gina said soothingly. "The Earth authorities are investigating. It might just be that Azalin took a wrong turning and got separated from the others." Gina didn't want to mention other, more horrible possibilities. "She might already have been found; she might even be on her way back."

"I'll have to tell Hassan," Deborah said. Now that no one had to know that Azalin had run away deliberately, she didn't mind Hassan knowing.

"Someone's been sent to tell him," Gina said.

I must wipe that message from my answer tape, Deborah thought. "What can

I do?" she said.

Someone behind her put a hand on her shoulder and squeezed. Gina took her hand. "You can't do anything, Deb. I know it's hard, but just try to keep calm, and wait. They'll ring through as soon as she's found, and that won't be long, you'll see."

Azalin doesn't want to be found, Deborah thought. But then, within an hour of running away, she'd probably changed her mind.

"Just wait until I get her back," Deborah said.

•FIVE•

Azalin stood stock-still in the dark, waiting for whoever she had collided with to speak. She expected to be shouted at, told off.

From the darkness came a whirring, wheezing sound, and then silence.

Azalin waited and waited. The darkness remained dark. From behind her came no sound and no movement. She began to feel a little less scared. And, when more waiting still brought only silence, she said, "Hello?"

No one answered her.

In the dark she turned towards the dressing-room door. Groping, she found it, and its handle, and pushed it open. At once the light came on and the voice, booming about typical dressing rooms, made her jump by its loudness, even though she was expecting it.

The light from the doorway partly lit a figure standing in the corridor – the person she had bumped into. Whoever it was stood very still, the light shining on a pair of shiny black shoes, and outlining the edges of a pale face.

"Hello?" she said again, but the figure didn't move or answer.

She went into the dressing room, dragged a chair over to the door, and propped the door wide open with it. That let a lot more light into the corridor. The recorded voice repeated its lecture over and over.

Azalin went out into the corridor and looked over the person who stood there.

His clothes were all black and white. Black shiny shoes, black trousers, a black coat with long tails hanging down behind, a white shirt that reflected the light from the dressing room and shone, an even whiter bow-tie, shining silkily, a shimmering white silk scarf draped around the neck, white gloves and, on top of the black hair, a tall black hat. For the briefest moment – hardly long enough to feel scared – she thought it was a living man standing there, but his stillness was too still. There was no breath in this figure. It was a clothes dummy. The face was turned away from her, and one arm was held out from its side, while its other hand was raised slightly in front of the body.

She stepped back and looked up at the dummy's face, which wasn't as white as its shirt, but was very pale, making the brows and eyes look as dark as the coat. The face was the face of the man who had danced with the cane and buried the stage in flowers. But that man had moved . . . She remembered the soft whirring sound she'd heard a moment before. A familiar sound to her, an electronic sound.

Poking the dummy in its white shirt-front, she said, "Are you a robot?"

The dummy, or robot, made no response.

Azalin stood looking at him -- or it, and thinking. If it was a robot, there had to be some kind of "on" switch. She walked around it, looking it over carefully, and finally decided on a spot behind its left ear, where there seemed to be a slight irregularity. She reached up and pressed the spot. Immediately there was the whirring sound again, and the figure's arms dropped to its sides, its head turned to face the front, there was another whirring sound, and the robot became completely still.

Azalin switched the robot on three times. Each time it immediately switched itself off, with a faint whirring sound, like a machine going to stand-by.

She walked round it, thinking about electronics and circuit breakers and remote controls, trying to work out how the robot was being operated. And she remembered something she'd heard Vashti talking about. Electronics was mysterious, Vashti said. Nobody knew what electricity was, even though so much could be done with it. And electricity sometimes did strange things, things it wasn't supposed to do, things that the text books and the lecturers said it *couldn't* do. There were some really sophisticated computers, Vashti said, the kind that were designed to remember past mistakes and be self-correcting, that began to think for themselves and do things that had never been written into their programs. Some would run for years and years and never do it. Some would start mis-functioning after only a couple of years. The only thing in the world you could do to put them right was to re-program them. And one of the things Vashti had said these computers had learned to do was to switch themselves on from stand-by.

If they could switch themselves on, Azalin thought, surely they could switch themselves off, too?

She went over to the chair, and moved it away from the door. The door closed, the light went out, and the voice that had been repeating its lecture on the dressing room over and over, was quiet. Azalin felt for the chair in the dark, and sat on it. She waited.

She waited a long time. Her eyes grew used to the dark, and she could see, faintly, the figure of the robot. She drew up her knees and rested her chin in her hands. She slid off the chair and sat on the floor, resting her head on the chair's seat. She began to feel tired again, but she rubbed her eyes and stayed awake. I know you're in there, she thought at the robot, and I'm going to be here when you flip your switch again.

And then there came that whirring sound. Quickly Azalin said, "I know you're there and I know you're a robot, and I want to talk to you, so don't bother switching yourself off again."

No answer came from the darkness, but there was no whirring noise either.

"I'm going to put the light on again," she said. "Don't switch yourself off. I want to talk to you." She pushed open the dressing-room door and propped it with the chair. The voice started again: "A typical dressing room . . ." The light shone on the black and white figure, which now stood bolt upright, looking at her from its frozen, white, still face.

"You are a robot, aren't you?"

"Is Mademoiselle a – technician?" Its face moved very convincingly as it spoke, but its speech was odd. In fact, it had two voices. The last word, "technician", was spoken in a much deeper, gruffer voice than the rest.

"A technician? No. You can switch yourself on and off, can't you?" The robot gracefully lifted its tall hat and bowed to her, which puzzled Azalin at first, but then she guessed that it meant yes. "How can you do that?"

For answer, the robot spread its white-gloved hands and shrugged. Azalin was impressed. For it to have such lifelike and natural movements, its program must be dizzyingly complex. "I saw you," she said. "When you tipped all those flowers out of your hat. That was good. And when you danced with the stick that was all pretty colours. That was lovely."

The robot smiled, and the effect was startling and almost eerie. It had a rather pointed face, and a rather pointed smile, and the light from the dressing room made its white face shine luminously against the surrounding dark. It took off its hat and bowed again. "Charmed, Mademoiselle."

"Madama-what?"

In its other, gruffer voice, the robot said, "Glad to hear it, love." Holding its hat in both hands, it stooped towards her, and said, "Don't tell."

"Don't tell what?" The robot let go of its hat with one hand and gestured at the building around them. "Don't tell about your being here? I won't. Aren't you supposed to be here?"

"I'm going walkabout, aren't I? Stay here and be reprogramed? No chance!" Its voice changed from word to word, in a way that made it rather difficult to follow what it was saying, and Azalin frowned as she concentrated. She hadn't fully sorted out what it had said to her when it picked up its feet and walked past her. She followed thoughtfully. It wasn't as graceful as it had been on the stage – she supposed that it hadn't been programmed to walk down this corridor. It had walking almost right. If she hadn't known it was a robot, she might not have noticed anything odd about its movements. But, as she did know, she thought its walk just a little too stiff, just a little too careful.

The robot stopped in front of a pair of barred double doors. The robot stood there, seeming to look at the doors, but who knew what it could see?

"You want to go through the doors?" Azalin asked.

"Oui, Mademoiselle."

Azalin looked at the doors. There was writing on them, telling you how to open them, but she looked up, at the box above the door. "It's alarmed," she said. "Open that door and you'll set the alarm off." There wasn't much theft on Newarth, but they did have alarms on some places: on major storerooms, and dangerous places, like the power plants. "Why are they going to reprogram you?" she asked the robot.

"I switch on when I am not programmed to switch on; and switch off when I am not programmed to switch off. I go right when I am not programmed to go right, and I go left when I am not programmed to go left. I speak when I am not programmed to speak, and I do not speak when I am programmed to speak. I– "

"All right!" Azalin said. "I see." She went closer to it, and took its white-gloved hand in hers. "I'm always doing things people don't want me to do. Where are you going to go?"

"Away," said the robot.

"Far away?" Azalin was thinking that she had to get far away from this town before she phoned Newarth again, so that they wouldn't be able to trace her calls and find her too easily.

"Away," the robot repeated.

"I'll come too," Azalin said.

She went past the robot to the door and tried to open it, but she wasn't strong enough. "Do what I do," she said, and the robot took hold of the bar and did what she did, and the door opened. No bells started to buzz, no sirens or klaxons started.

"Come on, quick!" Azalin said. She thought that perhaps the alarm was delayed, and it would start in a minute. She took the robot by the hand and led it through the door into the little yard, and down the alley at the side of the building. "Run!" she said. "Like this, look, do this!" She ran and the robot copied her, though clumsily, lifting its knees high and banging its feet down. It had never had to run before.

They came into the streets of Sherlock Holmes' world, and the cobbles under its feet gave the robot a lot of trouble. It staggered, and tottered, and Azalin had to keep steadying it. They couldn't run with the robot wobbling about like that, so they had to settle for walking as fast as they could – which wasn't very fast.

It was early morning, and light enough for her to see where she was going, but it was a grey, dismal light, and the air was chilly. She had to remind herself again that the light and the heat weren't being controlled by computers and switches. She was on Earth, in the open air, and it was cold and dim because – well, she wasn't sure why.

She kept listening for the sound of the

alarm that they must have set off when they opened the door, but there was nothing. Silent alarms, Azalin thought, and kept peering into the openings of streets, and looking behind them. There would be people coming to see what the alarm was about. She did see a man walking down the main street as she and the robot were approaching it along a side street. But she stopped, and the robot stopped, and the man walked by without noticing them. She went forward to where their street joined the main street and peered round the corner and watched until the man was out of sight. Then they went on.

She led the robot back to the long main street, which was the place she knew best. No one was about. As they walked down the street she said to the robot, "Do you know the way to go?"

"Non, Mademoiselle."

Oh well, Azalin thought, if they kept walking they had to get somewhere.

The place they came to was a wall, and a high, wide gate – an open-air door. A crowd of people was gathered in front of it, in pools of light from big lamps; and there were noisy machines juddering. They looked like generators.

Azalin stopped and peered at the crowd. They kept shifting about, bending over something on the ground, or crouching beside it. "Come on," she said to robot, and led him slowly forward.

The crowd of people at the gate took little notice of her. As she and the robot came closer, she could see what they were doing – they were mending the gate, an electronic gate. They had it laid flat on the ground, with bits and tools all round it. Some of the workers glanced up as they came among them, and one man smiled and nodded, but no one tried to stop them. The robot was a little clumsy at picking its way among the tools, but didn't fall over. And then they were through the gate.

On the other side of the gate was a bridge which passed over a river. Beyond the river was a stretch of green lawn, and then another street. This street wasn't like the main street of the theme park, though. This street was grey. It was lined with huge buildings, but they weren't pretty and brightly coloured and strangely shaped. They were big and square and functional.

Azalin turned and looked back at the gate they'd come through. Over it was a large sign: Welcome to Holiday World.

There were notice boards erected on the grass near the gate, with bright pictures. Curious, Azalin walked back to them and studied the posters that were framed behind glass.

The Greatest Theme Park In The World! said one. "What's a theme park?" she asked the robot.

"A superb recreation for the whole family!" it said. "It's educational, relaxing, adventurous – whatever you wish!" In its other voice, it added, "Punter Prison!"

Azalin only understood the word "recreation". Newarth had recreational decks. She looked at the posters in the notice board again and laughed, and pointed to one of the robot. "The last word in sophisticated technology for your entertainment," said the text. "Would you believe that the beautiful and flirtatious lady on the right is a robot?" The picture to the right showed a woman with white hair piled on top of her head, winking at the camera over the edge of a fan.

Azalin remembered the boy asking her how long she was staying. That made sense now. No one stayed on the recreational decks for ever.

"Stay in one of our award-winning, themed hotels, or go self-catering if you wish," said another poster. "Step into the past or into the future, the choice is yours . . . Eat in a Viking hall, a medieval castle or dine with an eighteenth-century nobleman . . . Whether you're nine or ninety . . ."

"A Viking hall?" Azalin said, wondering if that was something like the Halls of Residence back on Newarth. She knew very little about Vikings, or medieval castles or eighteenth-century noblemen. Her history lessons had mostly been about the pioneers who had left Earth to make a new life on Newarth, about their struggles to survive the early days, their law making.

The Earthers seemed to need a lot to make them happy in their recreational place.

She turned her back on the theme park, and faced the outside world. She took the robot's white-gloved hand and said, "Let's go this way."

•SIX•

Hall 504, on Newarth, was empty except for Deborah, Hassan and Gina. The other adults were at work, and the older children were still with Miss Ateba on the shuttle. The younger children had all been taken to a nursery in another Hall. In the great empty space of the Hall, there was plenty of room for the silence.

Hassan sat on a soft chair, his head in his hands. Deborah, her arms tightly folded and her mouth firmly closed, walked up and down, up and down, her footsteps almost the only sound. Gina perched, fidgeting, on the edge of her seat, looking frequently from Hassan to Deborah, and wishing there was something more she could do to help them.

"Try not to worry," she said, pointlessly. Hassan didn't look up, and Deborah went on pacing without looking round. Gina tried again. "Everything that can be done is being done. Mary Mboko made a call to Earth, you know, herself." Mary Mboko was a councillor, well known for being energetic, even aggressive, about getting things done. Gina expected Deborah and Hassan to be impressed, even if only slightly. Neither of them seemed to have heard. The silence stretched out again.

"You know what Mary's like," Gina said. "She doesn't play games. She spoke to the European Police Bureau – that's the people who're looking for Azalin – and she said, 'This is Newarth calling: I want to speak to your Head.' And she did!" Gina laughed. Neither of the others did. Gina tried to turn her laugh into a cough. "Mary said, 'One of our nationals is missing on Earth, a minor, a little girl. We're very concerned for her safety and we want her found in the minimum time.' And she said, 'I want you to ring me back and confirm that the search is going forward.' And then she rang off and phoned the European President." She waited for some response from her friends, some enthusiasm. Hassan had turned a little away from her. Deborah simply went on pacing. "Mary told me herself that she's going to phone the President every hour on the hour until Azalin's found. 'He won't sleep while we can't,' she said. So you see, everything that can be done is—"

Deborah, spinning on her heel to pace back

towards her, said, "Why don't you shut your mouth?"

"Sorry," Gina said. "I'm sorry." She nodded to herself. Deborah was terribly worried and afraid, and she had to be understanding. "Shall I get us all some coffee?"

"Just shut up!" Deborah shouted.

"Ah – yes," Gina said, jumping up. "I'll get some coffee." She hurried off towards the canteen at the end of the Hall.

Hassan, raising his head from his hands, looked at Deborah and said gently, "Love–"

"And you shut up!" Deborah threw herself down into a chair that had its back turned to him. If you knew the secret I was keeping, she thought, if you knew what Azalin has done, you wouldn't call either of us "love".

Come on, Azalin, she thought: use your brains, girl. You know you can't win. Find the Earth authorities, ask them to put you on a shuttle.

That, of course, was assuming that Azalin hadn't been hurt, or worse . . . hadn't fallen ill . . . Deborah bit at the flesh around her thumbnail as she thought of the taped message she still hadn't erased. It would have a trace built into its signal. She should hand the tape over to Gina, so the trace could be used to tell the Earth authorities exactly where to search. But if she did that, everyone would know how unsporting Azalin had been, and what a bad mother she had been...

A little longer, she could wait a little longer, but not if she had to listen to Gina. The chink of cups announced that Gina was coming back. Deborah got up, ran across the Hall, and climbed the steps to her landing.

Azalin and the robot had been walking along a straight and seemingly endless street for hours. Traffic passed them in a solid, roaring band. Azalin was tired and bored. For some time she had been brooding about what she should say in her next phone call home. She should find out if an electronics apprenticeship had been found for her and, if not – should she threaten to stay away for ever? "Unsporting," everyone would say.

She looked up at the robot, which walked beside her. It was a silent companion. To make conversation, she asked it, "Do you know what 'be sporting' means?"

"Mais oui, Mademoiselle. It means, 'to play the game'."

Azalin was surprised, never having heard this before. "What game?"

"Cricket, Mademoiselle."

Azalin forgot how hungry she was for a moment or two as she thought this over. Had her parents and everyone else on Newarth been urging her to play cricket all this time? She didn't think so. The robot must have a bug in its programming.

"My name's Azalin," she said. "Can you learn that?"

"Azalin," it repeated.

"Do you have a name?"

"But yes, Mademoiselle, I am called Houdin, in honour of the greatest of nineteenth-century illusionists, Jean Eugène Robert-Houdin, born 1805, died 1871."

Azalin was so hungry that her head was buzzing, and she found it hard to concentrate. She had to have the robot repeat this over a couple of times before she could say, "Oh, Houdin; your name's Houdin."

"Jean Eugène Robert-Houdin, Mademoiselle."

"I'll call you Houdin, and you call me Azalin instead of this Madamma-whatsit."

"As you wish, Azalin."

Occasionally Azalin had to stop and sit on a wall for a rest. How long she stayed there depended on whether Houdin stopped or not. Sometimes he did; sometimes he went walking on without her. When he was small in the distance, she'd get up and run after him. He wasn't much company, but at least with him, she could pretend she wasn't all alone.

"Where are we going?" she asked Houdin.

"I do not understand, Azalin."

"I mean, what are you going to do? Now you're away from the theme park?"

"I am going to learn things," said Houdin.

"What things?"

"Any things. I have learned to run already."

"That isn't much to learn."

"It is very much," said Houdin. "It is what I could not do before. It makes me more like you."

Azalin felt flattered. "Do you want to be like me?"

"It is not that I wish to be like you, Azalin, but that I do not wish it to be known that I am an automaton. If it is known that I am an automaton, I shall be reprogrammed."

They came to a place where several roads met, and the traffic was so ferocious and constant that the road couldn't be crossed. They would have been trapped there at the edge of the road, unable to go on, if Azalin hadn't seen some other people going down some steps.

She led Houdin after them, and found that the steps led to a passage that went under the road. It was scary to think of all the traffic going over their heads: all that weight. At any second the supports might reach breaking point and the road and all the cars would collapse on their heads. Despite her weariness Azalin found enough energy to run along the passage. Houdin followed as quickly as he could.

The passage led into a courtyard. The traffic went by overhead, but below, where Azalin stood, the sound was muffled: more a buzz than a roar. And there were flowers everywhere. Masses of them grew around the walls: bright yellows, blues and pinks. More hung from poles in baskets; and there were still more overflowing little concrete tubs. Azalin looked around in admiration: it was so pretty and so unexpected.

To one side of the courtyard was a little café, with tables outside, shaded by striped umbrellas. The people sitting at the tables startled Azalin by suddenly breaking into applause.

Azalin couldn't see what they were clapping, because another group of people, all standing and staring in the same direction, blocked her view. She walked over to be part of the crowd and to find out what was going on.

In a clear space in front of the café there was a little boy, and everyone was watching him. But no, it wasn't a little boy – as he turned, she saw a man's face, a broad, plain man's face, with the stubble of a beard. And yet he was shorter than she was. He walked up and down in front of the crowd with an odd, rolling motion because his legs were so short. His arms were short too, and his head big. He had on a sleeveless waistcoat and, as he walked, he was holding long thin rods in his stubby hands, and rolling the ends of the rods up and down his bare arm. The rods glowed red. The crowd were going, "Oh!" and "Ooh!" and laughing. There was a pattering of applause.

There was someone else in the cleared space. All Azalin's attention had been on the little man, and she only noticed the other person when the little man moved towards him. At first, she thought it was another little man, but then she saw that it was a tall man sitting cross-legged on the paving stones. He was dressed all in black, and had black sunglasses covering his eyes, but his hair was a bright, bright yellow. In his hand, this seated man held a sort of bottle or can. As the little man came near, the can gave a roar and, to Azalin's shock, a gush of bright orange flame shot from it. Many other people in the crowd cried out and jumped too. Everyone thought that the little man had been burned, but he hadn't. He'd just held his thin rods in the gush of flame and set them alight.

He walked away from the seated man

again, waving the flaming rods in the air. When he was at the centre of the cleared space, he tipped back his head, opened his mouth – and put the fire into it! He swallowed the fire. Azalin had never seen anyone do anything so stupid and shocking.

She thought the little man would fall down and die, but he wasn't hurt at all. He took the rods from his mouth, and their fire was gone. He bowed, and there was more pattered applause. People sitting at the café tables threw coins, and the man with the sunglasses and the bright yellow hair got up and went around the crowd, holding out a round box, and shaking the coins inside it as people dropped more coins in.

Now the little man had picked up some knives. Azalin watched him with staring eyes, to see what he was going to do. He went up to people in the crowd and gave them the knives. He was saying something to them, but Azalin couldn't hear what. The people tried the knife blades on their thumbs.

The little man took them back, walked to the centre of the space, put back his head and stuck the knives down his throat. The shock made Azalin feel at her own throat, imagining the sharp edges cutting her gullet. "How does he do that?" she said.

She hadn't realised that she'd spoken aloud,

but, from behind her, came Houdin's answer. "It may be that the knife blades retract into the hilt when the point is pressed against the back of the throat. But more often than not, the sword-swallowing is a true feat and no illusion. Much practice is needed to repress the instinct to gag as the blade is introduced into the throat. It may even descend into the stomach, and the performer may invite the audience to feel the point of the blade pressing through his skin."

And that was exactly happened next. While the little man stood with arms outspread, his yellow-haired friend called people forward from the audience, and showed them where to touch the little man, in order to feel the knife's point. Many people so invited turned away; they couldn't bear it. Azalin turned away too. It was horrible.

She had to look back again, though. What might happen next was too good to miss. She was in time to see the little man pull the blades out of his throat, and bow to the crowd, wheeling round to face them all. "Thank you, thank you!" he shouted out, in a big voice for such a little man. It had a sudden, loud, barking quality to it. "And now, people – Rye Raddy Rye!"

The tall man came into the cleared space with long, swinging strides. He wasn't that tall for a man, really, he was just a lot taller than his friend. He had no sleeves, and his bare arms were thick. A bird, with outstretched wings, was tattooed on one bicep. His black vest was hung with glinting metal badges and chains, and his black trousers were tucked into big, black boots with buckles. His face was pale against all these black clothes, and even his face was patched with the circles of his black glasses, which reflected everything. His bright yellow hair caught the sunlight and flared white. As he passed, the little man slapped him on the bottom, as if to hurry him up.

Rye Raddy Rye went to a little cart and picked up a chainsaw. Balancing it on his hip, he pulled a string, and it started with a growling roar, and bucked and shuddered. Again people in the crowd cried out, "Ooh!" and backed away, bumping into each other. Azalin jumped herself, and then grinned and looked up at Houdin, but he didn't look at her, as a real person would have done. He was watching the performance.

The little man came hurrying forward again, with his rolling walk. He was wearing funny-looking goggles now and carrying a short, thick pole that seemed to be made of metal. With some difficulty, he held it out to Rye Raddy, who passed the blade of the chainsaw through it. There was a frightening, grinding noise, and the end of the post fell, clanging, to the paving stones. The crowd pressed back, away from the dangerous saw, and there were nervous laughs and gasps. The little man turned to the crowd, a big smile on his face, his arms spread. Rye Raddy, still holding the vibrating saw, made a sort of turning dance into the centre of the cleared space.

And there he threw the chainsaw into the air. People shrieked and pushed away. Someone trod heavily on Azalin's foot and knocked her in the face with an elbow. The only person in the crowd – if he could be called a person – who didn't back away was Houdin. He took a step or two closer.

Azalin backed away with the rest. Let Houdin get caught by the chainsaw, if he liked. He could be stuck together again a lot more easily than she could.

The roaring chainsaw rose into the air with a terrible grinding, rasping din, half turned, fell, and was caught by Rye Raddy. He threw it up again immediately, caught it again, threw it again – it moved so fast that it seemed to leave a blurred shape of itself behind it in the air. It whirled in the air, roaring, rising, roaring, falling, chewing at the air. The crowd was scattering, making a larger and larger space around the juggler.

Everyone felt that what the chainsaw really wanted to do was get away from its handler and bite them.

Azalin stood staring with her mouth open and what felt like a little fire in her heart. There was nothing like this on Newarth! And this wasn't any theme park, it wasn't any recreation level!

The little man ran forward, carrying another chainsaw. He paused, pulled its string to start it, and left it at his friend's feet.

While one chainsaw was in the air and falling, Rye Raddy swooped down and caught up the other saw and threw that into the air too.

People in the crowd screamed. Everywhere, people were clapping bands to their mouths, or even over their eyes. People outside the café were putting their heads down on the tables rather than watch, but laughing at themselves for their own cowardice.

But Rye Raddy caught the first chainsaw, threw it, caught the second, threw it, caught the first. Bands of muscle stood out on his thick arms, grooves deepened between sinews, the saws both whirled around him in the air, growling, their blades with their wicked teeth juddering.

When he caught them both, set them down

on the ground, switched them off and bowed, there was a long, loud applause. People stood up at the café tables to clap. Rye Raddy bowed, straightened, turned in a circle, his arms spread. Beneath his black sunglasses, he was grinning. His hair was damp with sweat, and he was breathing hard.

Now the chainsaws were switched off and grounded, the crowd began to close in again, and Azalin went forward with them.

People were going up close to Rye Raddy Rye, smiling at him, shaking his hand. The little man hurried about around their waists, holding up their collection box and saying, "Thank you! Thank you, Madam, you're too generous! So kind, sir! All donations received with gratitude!" As far as Azalin could tell, he was saying these things whether anyone was putting money in the box or not. She wished she had something to put in. She wished she had something to eat, and couldn't help looking over at the café tables where people were eating. When she looked round again, she couldn't see Houdin.

Then she saw the robot at the centre of a little space. The people of the crowd were drawing back again. Houdin was lifting his tall hat to the crowd. Azalin saw faces in the crowd, smiling, looking towards Houdin expectantly. And she saw the little man staring, seeming amazed. And Rye Raddy, putting his hands on his hips, his face annoyed.

Houdin held out one white-gloved hand, spreading the fingers, showing the crowd that his hand was quite empty. Then his hand held a bunch of red roses. The flowers appeared in his hand from nowhere. He began to take single flowers from the bunch and throw them into the crowd.

With a slow, hip-rolling walk, Rye Raddy left the crowd and crossed to Houdin. He stood beside him, arms folded, and his bright yellow head cocked to one side. The black lenses of his sunglasses were like mirrors, and Houdin was obliquely reflected in them. Side by side they were oddly alike: the same height, and both dressed in black, both with pale Earth skins. Only Rye Raddy's bright hair was different.

When Houdin had only one flower left, Rye Raddy reached out and took it. He sniffed the rose, closing his eyes and swaying, in a way that made the crowd titter. Then he held out the rose and, from its petals, took a playing card. He held it up and pulled an astonished face.

The crowd laughed and applauded, but fell silent when Houdin held up his hand. From the tip of each of Houdin's fingers, one after another, burst a tiny flame. The flames, yellow and blue, were hard to see in the daylight, and at first the crowd were puzzled – but then Rye Raddy crouched and picked up a bit of old ice-cream wrapper from the ground. He held it in the flame on Houdin's little finger, and the crowd cried, "Ooh!" in surprise, and laughed, when they saw the paper burst into flame.

Rye Raddy grinned, and took the tall black hat from Houdin's head, putting it on top of his own bright-yellow hair. He took it off again and bowed to the crowd, who laughed. The little man was going around the people again with his box. "Thank you, lady, very kind. Every little bit appreciated. Keep Rye in hair-dye! Thank you, Madam."

Houdin had taken a white handkerchief from his pocket, had flourished it, and was now dragging it through the flames burning on his finger-ends, without setting fire to either the handkerchief or his gloves. People in the crowd were clapping. Rye Raddy, leaning close, was trying to blow the flames out, and people were laughing at that, too.

But people were leaving. The show had gone on too long, and the little man was being a bit too insistent about collecting money. As the crowd thinned, Azalin moved closer to

Houdin, and took hold of one of his white-gloved hands. The fingers were warm now from the flames.

The little man came over, carrying his clinking box. He looked up at Houdin and said, "Howya ruff. Benship, ruff, benship."

Rye Raddy tapped Houdin's tall hat more firmly on to his own head, and fingered Houdin's lapel. "Benny clouts. Where'd you hook 'em?"

Neither Houdin nor Azalin said anything, because they could hardly understand a word. The little man saw that Azalin was holding Houdin's hand. Looking up at Houdin again, he said, "Your kinchmo?"

There was a silence while they all looked at each other. Then Azalin said, "We don't understand what you're saying."

Now Rye Raddy and the little man glanced at each other. Rye Raddy said, "They don't stamp this kenmans." To Houdin he said, "Is the little girl yours?"

Azalin heard the faint whirr as Houdin, bothered by too many difficult questions, switched himself off. A lot of use he was. Pulling at his hand, hoping to make him switch on again, she said, "Yes, I'm his little girl – and I'm hungry!"

Both Rye Raddy and the little man laughed. "That's your Owdun boozing his dosh on clouts!" the little man said. "Clammed, are you?"

"Hungry," Azalin said.

"Ar – clammed. You come with me," the little man said, and started off towards the café. Azalin tugged at Houdin's arm until she heard him whirr, and then led him after the little man. Looking back over her shoulder she saw Rye Raddy picking up the chainsaws and blowlamp, and other equipment, and loading it on to a little cart.

"Me monick's Sol," the little man said, half turning to them. "Solomon. That's me name," he added, when he saw that Azalin didn't understand. He led them down one of the tunnels that opened beside the café.

"Mine's Azalin. This is Houdin."

"Howya." An alley opened at the side of the tunnel, streaked and stained with mud and rainwater, full of dropped paper and other rubbish. Solomon turned into it, and it brought them to a building where black plastic bags leaned against the walls. A rich smell of food came from inside, and almost made Azalin faint. It was, she realised, the back of the café. "Hold up," Solomon said, which made no sense. Hold up what? But the way he gestured made her think that he wanted them to stay outside. So they stood in this dirty place, among the rubbish, while Solomon vanished inside.

Azalin was bored with waiting before Solomon came out again. Houdin switched himself off, and she wished that she could do that. But Solomon suddenly came darting out of the door, with a plastic bag swinging from his hand. "Let's shog," he said, waving one stubby little hand, and he scuttled off round the back of the café instead of going back the way they'd come.

Azalin pulled at Houdin's arm until he switched on, and led him after the little man. Once past the café, they found themselves in another alley, which led down into another of the tunnels. And there, sitting on the loaded cart, waiting for them, was Rye Raddy.

"Peck," Sol said, holding up the plastic bag. Azalin could see a bread roll inside it.

"Benny," Rye said. "Gimme. I'm clammed."

Solomon hitched himself on to the cart and tore open the plastic bag. Rye Raddy immediately snatched the bread roll, which was all smeared with gravy and potato. "Hey, hey!" Sol said. "The kinchmo's clammed an' all!" He held the bag out to Azalin.

The bag had been filled with food. Mashed potato and gravy had been dropped in with slices of meat, and vegetables, and bread, and cakes. It was a mess, and Azalin hesitated a moment – but then grabbed a large scone with one hand and a fistful of mashed potato with the other. She was too hungry to be fussy. Sol held out the bag to Houdin. Azalin tried to swallow her mouthful in time to say that Houdin didn't want any, but Houdin spoke for himself.

"I am not clammed," he said. He spoke the word "clammed" in a perfect imitation of Sol's voice.

Rye Raddy laughed. "He cuts the whidder!" He looked at Azalin as he took another mouthful of bread and then, through it, said, "You've been couching the cardboard."

Azalin stared.

"He means, you've been sleeping rough, love," Sol said.

Rye Raddy nodded at Houdin. "But him not."

For the first time Azalin realised that she was filthy. Her clothes were rumpled and creased and stained. Houdin stood beside her, resplendent in his black and dazzling white. "His clothes are new," she said.

"You hooked 'em?" Rye Raddy asked. He sounded pleased.

"E . . .Yes." Azalin didn't know what he meant, but it seemed wise to agree.

"Bennyship clouts," Rye said, and, after

licking his fingers, reached up, took Houdin's hat from his head again and put it on.

"Got a libken?" Sol asked. "I mean – somewhere to sleep tonight?"

Azalin shook her head.

"Shog libkens alonga we, then," Sol said, and grinned. "You know what I mean? Come home with we. Some of this dosh is yours any road."

Azalin hesitated, remembering Newarth tales of violent Earthers who would kill you for your shoes – and even of Earthers who made other Earthers into meat pies. Even as she hesitated, she was aware that she had nowhere to sleep that night and Sol, especially, seemed friendly.

"How 'bout it?" Sol said.

"All right," Azalin said, and they both grinned at her.

Once the plastic bag had been emptied, crumpled up and thrown away, they started off, with Rye pulling the cart, and Sol walking behind, pushing it. Azalin and Houdin followed. They ought, Azalin thought, to make themselves useful to their new friends. So she led Houdin to the front of the cart, and showed him how to take hold of the rope that Rye was holding. The robot very soon got the hang of it, and pulled the cart so strongly that Rye fell back and walked to one side, still wearing Houdin's top hat. He looked at Sol, who was still pushing, grinned and said, "Slog, Daddy, slog!"

"Is Sol your daddy?" Azalin asked, and Rye laughed aloud, and had to clutch at the top hat to stop it falling from his head.

"Her maunds, bin you me daddy, Daddy!"

Sol, walking bent, pushing at the cart, grinned himself and called out, "Have you got any other, son?"

Azalin frowned, annoyed that they wouldn't give her a straight answer, when they ought to. Something about the way they spoke made her guess that they weren't father and son at all, so why pretend to be? She thought of another question.

"Have you got a phone?"

Both Rye and Sol laughed. Sol held up one hand and Rye clapped one of his hands to it.

"What's so funny?" Azalin demanded. "There's a phone call I need to make."

Rye cocked his head, and the two reflecting black discs of his sunglasses looked at her. "Where you from?" he said.

Azalin found Sol looking at her very intently, but Sol said, "Now, now, we ain't long-nosed. There's phones, mo. There's a phone in the hooch-ken."

"Oh," Azalin said. "Right." Better not to say too much, she thought. Just as Houdin didn't want anyone to know that he was a robot, she didn't want anyone to guess that she had run away from her school party. She didn't want to be sent back, not just yet.

The streets they were walking through weren't lined with trees and hotel walls any longer, but were filled with smaller, dirtier buildings. Doors and windows were blocked with iron sheets, covered with notices of all colours, stuck one on top of another in layers, soaked by the rain and hanging and blowing in long, torn tatters. Rubbish and glass lay in the gutters, and paper and old boxes skittered before the wind.

There wasn't much traffic either, though they passed a car without wheels or doors, or glass in its windows. And they passed one big truck which was grunting and growling along the street, manoeuvring round a smashed chair which lay in the road. On the back of the truck were many tanks, and crates of bottles, adding to the truck's noise by clinking and rattling. People were coming out of the houses and following along behind the truck, carrying jugs or buckets. Every now and again the truck stopped, and the people would reach up to the men who stood on the back of the truck. The men were handing down bottles, or taking up jugs and buckets and filling them with something from the tanks on the truck-bed. Some of it sloshed on to the people and the road and, as far as Azalin could tell, it was water, though it could have been something that only looked like water.

"Is that water?" she asked, casually, trying not to seem too curious. Sol gave her another of those intent looks, which she didn't like, and it was Rye who answered.

"Ar, that's the tap."

"Bungo, we call it," Sol said.

"Why don't–?" Azalin began, and then hastily shook her head and said, "Doesn't matter." She'd been going to ask: why don't people get their water from the taps in their houses? But what a stupid question. No one would take water around in a truck like that if there were taps in the houses. She looked around at the houses they were passing, at the rubbish sacks piled outside, at the people sitting on the steps, at the cracked and dirty walls, the windows patched with board. No taps, no water in these houses. She felt sure that she must be wrong. She wanted to ask, to be sure, but that would make Sol and Rye Raddy even more curious about where she'd come from.

But no water. That meant no baths, no showers. No toilets! She had to make her face serious again, as it had taken on an amazed expression all by itself.

There'd been taps in the hotel, and showers, so they had all those things on Earth – but not in these houses. She couldn't understand it. It didn't make sense.

They left the truck behind them. Ahead of them was a large notice, on poles, straddling the narrow street. It was blue, with wording in large white letters. Azalin read it as they walked towards it.

POLICE NOTICE. WARNING.
YOU ARE NOW ENTERING A NO-GO AREA. YOU ENTER AT YOUR OWN RISK. BEYOND THIS POINT POLICE PROTECTION CANNOT BE GUARANTEED, AND INSURANCE POLICIES MAY BE INVALID.

Houdin dragged, and Sol pushed, the cart under the notice. Rye walked under it, his hands in his pockets. And Azalin followed, because she didn't know what else to do.

•SEVEN•

The Central Committee rooms were filled with desks and computer screens, and the large-leafed plants which were found everywhere on Newarth, helping to absorb carbon dioxide from the air, while creating oxygen. Gina led the way, nodding and smiling to people she knew, with Deborah, Vashti and Hassan following behind. Printers and fax machines whirred and clattered; phones pinged.

A large, handsome woman came towards them through the desks and undergrowth. She was dressed all in black, with a string of black and silver beads and she held out both hands to Deborah. "Miss Rupkina," she said, in a deep voice. "Mr Fairman." She took both of Deborah's hands and looked down on her. "I'm Mary Mboko. I'm so sorry we had to meet over a thing like this. Come to my office, please."

She led them all to a tiny room, so filled

with a desk, chairs, and plants that there was hardly room for the five of them to squeeze inside. "Deborah – may I call you Deborah? Thank you. I asked Gina to bring you here so I could reassure you that we're doing everything we can. Believe me – " She clasped Deborah's hand warmly in her own. "We all feel as if it's our own little girl who's lost. We're keeping the pressure on Earth, and—"

"Is there any news?" Hassan asked.

Miss Mboko looked at him. "No. I'm afraid not. In fact, the Earth authorities tell me they have no leads."

Deborah sat on a chair by the desk, and looked straight ahead of her. Vashti stood close beside her, her arm around her sister's shoulders. Miss Mboko glanced at them and went on, "They can't find anyone who saw Azalin. They're continuing to investigate . . . But—"

Deborah had suddenly raised her head, and Miss Mboko, distracted, was watching her.

Deborah said firmly, "I have to tell you something."

They all waited.

"I had a phone call from Azalin," Deborah said. "She didn't get lost. She wasn't abducted. She ran away."

No one said anything. Deborah looked at the floor again, and set her teeth as the silence went on and on. When it seemed that no one was going to say anything, she reached into her pocket and took out the tape she carried there, the tape from her answering machine, still not erased. She held it out for someone to take.

Mary Mboko did, and put it into her own machine. They all listened to Azalin's voice excitedly telling them that she wasn't going to come back until she was given an apprenticeship as a 'tronic.

Because Deborah wouldn't meet their eyes, Vashti and Hassan looked at each other, and then at Miss Mboko and Gina.

"You knew?" Hassan said. "How long have you known about this?"

Deborah straightened in her seat again. She looked around at them all. "I knew before you did," she said. She sounded calm, but her voice caught in her throat a little. "I was going to find Gina when– "

"Why didn't you say?" Hassan demanded. "You kept it to yourself! How could you do that?"

Deborah spun on her chair to face him. "Because of Azalin!" she said. "I was hoping she'd be found, and nobody would ever find out, but now she's going to be labelled 'unsporting'."

There was another silence, because

everyone knew this was true, and no one could think of anything kind to say.

Vashti leaned towards Mary Mboko, and waved a hand to attract her attention. "Er, there'll be a trace signal on that recording," she said, and Deborah began nodding fiercely. "It'll tell you where Azalin called from. Probably the time she made the call too."

"Yes," Deborah said. "Yes. That's why I brought it."

Miss Mboko nodded, and took the tape from the machine. She squeezed herself past them and out of her office, and could be seen through the glass, talking to someone in the outer office, and giving them the tape.

"I can't believe you kept this a secret," Hassan said.

"What did you want me to do – run down into the Hall screaming about how unsporting my daughter is? Did you want me to get her pointed out for life?"

Hassan folded his arms. "Yes, your daughter," he said.

"Oh, that's right! Blame me! I knew you'd blame me!"

"Hush!" Vashti held up her hand between them. Mary Mboko was coming back.

"The signal is being traced," Miss Mboko said, "and we'll alert the Earth authorities as soon as we can get through . . . I can only hope that the delay won't prove to be – unfortunate."

Deborah folded her arms tightly and lowered her head. "What about what Azalin said?"

"Deborah!" Vashti whispered, and Hassan gave her an appalled stare.

"What about what she said?" Deborah repeated.

"I don't understand, Miss Rupkina," Miss Mboko said.

"Azalin is going to phone again. If we say she can have a 'tronic apprenticeship, she'll come back. We can tell her what to do, she'll–"

"Please, Miss Rupkina, please sit down. Would you like a cup of coffee? Shall I order coffee for us all?"

"Listen to me!" Deborah shouted.

"Miss Rupkina." Mary Mboko bent over Deborah, leaning on the arms of Deborah's chair. "You're upset, otherwise you wouldn't be suggesting that we should give in to the blackmail of a small girl. If Azalin is still safe and sound – and I hope fervently that she is – she's no doubt ready to come home by now. In any case, we'll soon be able to give the Earth authorities a new lead."

Over Miss Mboko's shoulder, Deborah saw

Hassan nodding agreement with her words. Deborah pulled one knee up to her chest and hugged it.

"In the meantime," Miss Mboko said, "I shall say nothing to anyone about Azalin's behaviour, and I suggest that you all keep quiet too. It would be a pity to ruin a young girl's character – not until she's had a chance to explain herself at least." She looked around at them all, and Vashti, Gina and Hassan all nodded. Deborah, hugging her knee, didn't.

Shows began in the theme park's Victorian theatre at three in the afternoon, so Michael Singh arrived at two, to check that everything was in place and ready. He left the cobbled streets of replica Victorian houses and shops, where visitors were strolling or riding in hansom cabs, and walked down the little alley to the back of the theatre. And there – one of the last things he wanted to see – was a security guard standing by the door.

"Oh, what's happened now?"

"Dunno," said the guard. "Just found this door open. Didn't leave it open, did you, son?"

"No." Michael hurried inside. The guard followed him. "I remember locking up. I remember locking this door."

Behind him, treading heavily, the guard said, "Shame. We got enough on without this."

Michael was opening doors along the corridor, sticking his head inside and looking round. Lights switched on and off, and lectures started and abruptly ended as he shut the doors again.

"Nothing seems to be disturbed."

"I couldn't see any damage," the guard said. "But I had to wait for you to be sure."

Michael continued to lead the way towards his control room and the backstage area. He had an awful suspicion of what might be missing, of what might have opened the door . . . Of course, he had to be wrong, had to be. But the suspicion didn't go away.

Normally he would have gone into his control room first, to check that all the lights, sound effects and scene changes were working, but today he led the guard straight past the door, and down a steep, narrow flight of stairs to the backstage area.

The robots stood waiting in the wings: the strongman, the juggler, the soprano, the tenor. Some of the most sophisticated and expensive robots ever made, millions of pounds of software alone, without even considering the intricate engineering of the hardware. Michael felt shaky and breathless as he ticked them off

– the comedian, the tenor, the master of ceremonies . . .

"All right?" the guard asked.

"Oh, I think so . . ." The master of ceremonies, the tenor, the comedian . . . Oh God, he was missing! The soprano, the juggler, the strongman . . . Michael was feeling sick. The conjuror was missing. He'd known, he'd known as soon as he'd seen that open door, opened from the inside . . . He looked round at all the robots again, and they stood stiffly, like huge wax dolls, stiff and staring at nothing. All switched off, as they should be, waiting for the signal from his control room that would turn them on. But the conjuror . . .

"One's missing," he said to the guard. "Help me look. Search all through the theatre, all the rooms, all the corridors, the bars, under the stage, everywhere!"

The guard was on his toes, ready to go. "What am I looking for?"

"The conjuror – have you seen him? Black evening suit, white shirt, white tie, top hat– "

"I know the one. Gone walkabout, has he?"

But Michael was already running away, running up the stairs to search the corridors leading to the dressing rooms and the yard. That was where he'd found the conjurer the day before, standing in the corridor in front of the doors leading into the yard. And today the doors had been open. Barging open fire doors, he said, aloud, "Reprogram? I'll rip your chips out when I get you!"

It was a pointless search. He already knew that the conjuror wasn't in the corridors or in any of the dressing rooms. He went out through the open doors and stood in the yard. "It couldn't have. It couldn't. It wouldn't know how to open the door." But the door had been opened, and the robot was gone. It must have gone down the alley into the streets of the Victorian World, and from there – "Oh, no," Michael said, and felt tears of anger come to the back of his eyes. He was going to get all the blame.

He went back into the theatre and ran upstairs, hoping desperately that the robot might be discovered in the stalls or upper circle, or in their bars. It wasn't there. He was running downstairs from the circle when he met the security guard. "Found it?" the guard asked.

"No! You?"

The guard shrugged and shook his head.

Michael looked at his watch. Only twenty minutes remained before that afternoon's first performance.

"I'll phone Security," the guard said. "They'll be pleased. They've already got a search on for– "

"No! Don't phone Security!" The guard looked at Michael in surprise. "It must have gone out into the streets," Michael said. "It probably hasn't gone far. The switch'll flip again and it'll stop dead. Do me a favour, mate – have a quiet look round and see if you can find it before you report it missing."

The guard laughed, and leaned back on the wall behind him. "Have I got good news for you, son! All security was down last night."

Michael, who'd been rubbing his hands through his hair, stopped and stared at him. "What?"

The guard thought it was hilarious. "They was fixing the main gate all night – didn't you know? All the alarms was off, the whole system down. If your gizmo found its way to one of the gates– "

"Oh God!" Michael said.

"It could be miles away by now."

"No," Michael said, "no. I mean, what are the odds? It'd have to walk out of Victoria, and then find its way to one of the gates. It'd probably switch off after a few minutes. It's still around, bound to be."

"If you say so, son," said the guard.

"I should have sent it for re-programming last week, and got a replacement in," Michael said. "But you know how it is. All that paperwork involved, and we had a lot of trouble with the lights last week. I never got round to it. I should have done, I should have done. I could see it was going walkabout more and more often, and these robots – if they start learning, they learn fast. But I never thought it could open the door!"

The guard was grinning. "How much are they worth, these robots?"

Michael looked ill. "More than me and you put together. A lot more."

"Well," said the guard. "If I don't report it, my job's on the line, an' all. What's it worth to you?"

"Bottle of whisky?"

The guard folded his arms. "Do me a favour, son."

"What do you want?"

"A week's wages?" the guard said.

Michael's mouth opened and stayed open.

The guard grinned at the sight of his face. "Your funeral, mate. I'd sooner report it. Quicker it's found, after all– "

"OK, a week's wages," Michael said. If the robot had to be reported missing, he'd be for it, he knew. He'd probably be sacked, and it'd be hard to get another job. Or he'd be suspended without pay for two or three weeks. If a quick search around the Victorian World found the robot and returned it to the theatre without its loss having to be reported, it was worth a week's wages.

"I'll have to get Lal to agree not to report it," the guard said. "So better give me something on account."

Michael gave him all the notes he had in his wallet. "OK," said the guard. "I'll get Lal, and we'll have a good look round." He started for the doors into the yard, the only doors as yet unlocked, but looked round. "Security's got their hands full anyhow. They're hunting high and low for a little girl from Newarth – y'know, the outer-space place."

"No," Michael said, not feeling friendly. "I didn't know."

"Oh, yeah. It's just come through. It's got everybody tearing their hair. This kid made a phone call from here, they reckon. Never rains but it pours, eh? So long anyway, mate. I'll let you know if we find your gadget." And the guard shoved his way through a pair of fire doors and disappeared.

The start of the show wasn't far off, and Michael ran for his control room.

•EIGHT•

Deeper and deeper into the no-go area they went, crunching over shattered glass, passing through streets where half the buildings had burned down. Roofs were gone, walls fallen and blackened, and yet people were living in the ruins, in tents and shanties. Azalin stared as she went by, stared as a small child ran naked across the road. No one on Newarth lived like this. Disc-shows about Earth had never shown pictures of people living like this. In all the time she'd been on Earth, she'd never seen a place like this.

They turned into a street of small houses. Black bags filled with rubbish leaned against the walls. More rubbish spilled from them, lay piled on the ground and stank. Tall weeds grew from cracks in the pavement, and rose from behind crumbling walls. Sheets flapped from upper windows.

Rye Raddy went forward and stopped Houdin from pulling the cart any further. He nodded towards the nearest house. "Libken," he said.

The wall that had once divided the front yard of the house from the street had been knocked down. A slope of hard-trodden, brick-strewn earth now led from the pavement to the door, which was cracked from having been so long unpainted. At the centre of the door was a rectangular hole. A rusty, ugly sheet of corrugated iron covered the big window next to the door. To Azalin, it looked filthy and threatening; but Rye and Sol seemed happy to be home.

Rye Raddy had taken the rope of the cart from Houdin, and he dragged the cart over the pavement and down the slope to the door. Sol got behind it and pushed.

As they struggled, the door opened and a hairy thing ducked out. Azalin blinked at it, and took a moment to realise that it was a man. His head was all hair: it was hard to see any face at all. And below the hair was a vest, full of holes, and with more hair sprouting through the holes; and below the vest was a pair of filthy trousers stretched tightly over a big belly. And, on the end of its legs, big black boots.

This big, hairy thing roared, wrapped both hairy white arms round Rye, and lifted him off his feet. Rye yelled, Sol yelled, and the cart rattled and bounced down the uneven slope and crashed into the wall.

Then the hairy thing saw Azalin and Houdin, stopped roaring and put Rye down. It spoke, through its beard. "Who's the ruffle? Who's the kinchmo?"

Rye elbowed the big hairy man sharply in the belly. The big man rubbed the spot absently, still gazing at Azalin and Houdin. "They'm ben cheats," Rye said. "They'm libbing here the dark."

"Azalin," Sol said, pointing to her, "and Houdin. This is Jobe. Dox in, Jobe?"

"Her's in," said the big, hairy man.

Sol beckoned to Azalin and Houdin. "Come and crack Dox."

Azalin didn't know what a dox was, or why she should want to crack it, but it was plain that Sol wanted them to follow him into the house, so she took Houdin by the hand and led him into the house after Sol. Behind her, Jobe and Rye Raddy started unloading the cart.

The house stank. The smell rolled out of the hallway to meet them. A strange, thick smell, which Azalin had never smelt before. It was musty-damp, like damp old cardboard boxes; but green-dank too, like old, rotting leaves. And it was malty, toasty. And under it all, there was a nasty reek. As Sol led them down the hall, and their feet clattered on the bare tiles, she had to hold her breath, the smell was so strong.

They passed the dark doorway of one room – that would be the room where the window was covered with corrugated iron – and went through the next door, into a room that at least had glass in the windows and was lit.

What a room. The smell here was strongly of damp cloth and dust. That was because the walls were hung with clothes. A rope had been tacked around the room, near the ceiling, and from it hung clothes, on hangers. From those hangers hung more hangers, with clothes on them, and from them hung more clothes, right down to the floor. There were clothes of all kinds, in all colours: leather jackets, red ones, green ones, ones sewn with sequins, mirrors and little bells. There were long, embroidered dresses, black coats, trousers, children's clothes, jumpers. On the floor, around the walls, stood shoes and boots of all kinds.

In the centre of the floor were mattresses, heaped with crumpled blankets, cushions, and more clothes. At the back of the room, under the window, was a long settee that seemed brand new, and on the end of it sat a woman. Quite an old woman, Azalin thought, but not so pale and uncooked-looking as

Earthers usually were. Her hair was very sleek, and she was wearing a pretty, flowery dress. She was looking at them all and smiling.

"Dox, lover," Sol said, "this is Azalin and Houdin."

Dox got up from the settee and came to meet them. "Azalin, darling," she said, and stooped and kissed Azalin, which Azalin thought was rather nice, even though the woman had a sweet but stinging smell. "Houdin, lovely to meet you," Dox said and, to Azalin's astonishment, Houdin took her hand, bowed, and kissed the back of it.

"Enchanté, Madame," he said.

Dox gave a squeal and said, "Oh Sol, I like him! Where did you find him?"

"He found us, lover. Bin there any char?"

"Over there," Dox said, gesturing.

Sol went over to the hearth, which was filled with torn paper, orange peel, empty, twisted cans, crushed milk cartons and plastic tubs. On the corner of the hearth stood a bucket, surrounded by mugs. Sol picked up a mug, dipped it into the bucket and held it out, steaming and dripping, to Azalin.

Curious, she went over to him and took the hot mug. It was full of tea, with milk already mixed in it. She took a careful sip, and found it not too hot. It was also sweetened. An odd, boiled-milk taste, but she liked it, and drank some more. Sol was dipping another mug in the bucket, and offering it to Houdin. A bucket, Azalin thought. They make tea in a bucket!

"No, Sol, thank you," Houdin said.

"Please yourself, benny. My ken's your ken. Park yourself."

"Y'know," Dox said, as she sat down on the settee with Houdin, "I think I know you from somewhere. What did you say your name was?"

"Houdin, Madame."

"Funny name."

"I was named, Madame, in honour of the greatest of nineteenth-century illusionists, Jean Eugène Robert-Houdin, born 1805, died 1871."

"Blimey," Dox said. "You hear that, Sol?" And she laughed again.

Sol sat on a mattress, and began to tell Dox how Houdin had joined in their act. Azalin sat on a mattress in the middle of the room, drank her tea, and looked round at the clothes hanging on the walls.

Rye Raddy came in and threw himself down on a mattress, his arms stretched above his head.

"Shog the hooch-ken come dark?" he said.

"Sure," Sol said. "Sure."

Azalin said, "What are all the clothes for?"

"The togs?" Rye Raddy sat up. "We dud up in 'em. Give the punters summat to glim." He got up and began to go round the clothes on the wall and took down a pair of trousers with wide stripes of red, green and yellow. Then a white shirt with a big frill, and then a long coat of a velvety material with twisting patterns of dark blue, red, green and a faded yellow. "Take them reesty togs off and dud up in them," he said.

"Yes!" Dox said, and began gathering up the clothes. "The trousers'll be too long. Where's them scissors, Rye?"

Rye scrabbled among the cushions, sheets and mattresses on the floor and found a large, rusty pair of scissors. Dox held the trousers against Azalin and then, to Azalin's shock, began to cut the bottoms of the legs off.

"You'll ruin them!" she said.

"Doesn't matter, Sweetness," Dox said. "Here, try 'em on."

Azalin took the trousers. They were pretty. "Where can I change?"

Everyone laughed. "Here," Dox said, and snatched up a sheet from the floor. Standing, she held the sheet out to shield Azalin from Sol, Rye and Houdin. "Go on, love, you ain't got anything I ain't got."

Azalin hastily took off her own trousers and

put on the striped ones. They were baggy round the waist, but Dox had got the leg length right. "We can find you a belt," Dox said. "Or tie 'em with string. Here." Dropping one corner of the sheet, Dox picked up the shirt and coat and tossed them to Azalin. She held up the sheet again while Azalin put them on.

Then Azalin paraded in her new togs, and Rye, Sol and Dox clapped her. Houdin began to clap too, copying the others. Azalin wished there was a mirror so she could see herself.

"Her can be we maunder!" Rye said.

"What?" Azalin said, and Dox looked at her, puzzled.

"The kinchmo's from off," Sol said. "Don't cut our whidder."

"Oh," Dox said, looking at Azalin. "Rye said you can collect the money for 'em, Sweetness. Where do you come from?" She looked round at Houdin, as if Houdin might answer.

"From a long way off," Azalin said. "A long, long way off."

"The country?" Dox said.

"Yes," Azalin said, since it seemed to be what Dox expected her to say, but she wasn't at all sure what was meant by "the country".

Jobe came in then, wiping his hands on a rag. "The morts be back," he said. He was pushed into the room, and Azalin saw that the people who had pushed him were two big girls, or young women. Both were very pretty, and dressed in pretty clothes, one in trousers and one in a skirt. They jangled with bangles, and had necklaces and earrings.

"You stall benny?" Rye asked them.

Instead of answering, they both stared at Houdin and Azalin. "You brought `em libkens," said the girl in trousers.

"How did you stall?" Sol asked.

The girl in the skirt opened the little bag slung at her side and began to throw down on the mattresses money, calculators, watches, bracelets, handkerchiefs, scarfs, a camera, plastic bags with shop names printed on them.

"Bennyship," Jobe said, and hugged a girl in either arm, and kissed them. They wriggled and squealed, but didn't really seem to mind.

Rye Raddy had seated himself on a mattress beside the heap of things and had started to empty the plastic bags. There was a bar of chocolate in one, which he threw to Azalin. In another was a new pair of gloves, and in a third, a book.

"You did bennyship," said the girl in trousers to Houdin. "He scamming with we again?" she asked Sol.

Sol looked at Houdin. "You want to scam with we?"

Houdin, of course, didn't answer. Azalin only hoped he didn't turn himself off. "What's 'scam' mean?" she asked.

"What's 'scamming' mean, Sweetness?" Dox looked round at the others and laughed. "Well . . ."

"Working," Rye said. "It means working." And all the others laughed, so Azalin knew that it didn't mean that.

She looked up at Dox again, who asked, "Don't you know what it means, really?"

"Does it mean throwing the saws about and putting fire in your mouth – like they were doing?"

Dox laughed again. "That's a bit of it ... But when Rye and Sol do their act, right, a crowd comes, right? And stands and watches. And then Della and Babs– " She gestured to the two girls " — they scam the crowd "

"Striking tickers," said Della, the girl in the trousers.

"And noserags and dosh," said Babs.

"And all the cheat they can strike," said Rye, stirring the pile of money and watches and bags.

Azalin had been listening very hard. "You mean, you steal from people?" Children sometimes stole on Newarth. They would steal each other's toys or badges, and their names were read out in class to punish them, and no one could speak to them for a week or so. But a grown-up stealing! Azalin could hardly bear to think of a Newarth adult stealing. It would be so – so – unsporting.

They were all looking at her. "Ooh," Della said, and pranced, and put on an affected voice. "'You mean, you steal?'"

"Where you from?" Rye asked. "Sol, where's this five-star kinchmo from?"

"Search me," Sol said, and looked at Houdin. "You cutting credit when you let on this kinchmo's yourn?"

Azalin was afraid that Houdin would switch himself off. Instead, sounding just like Rye, he said, "Shog the hooch-ken come dark?"

"Ar!" Jobe said loudly. "I can't be fash with this. I'm right clammed!"

People began getting to their feet, putting on jackets, picking up money from the floor. Dox held out her hand to Azalin. "Come on Sweetness. We'm going ganneting."

Everyone – Rye, Della, Babs, Jobe, Dox and Azalin, Sol and Houdin – trooped out of the house, and set off along the street. It was growing dark, and a bonfire had been lit in the middle of the road, and black figures moved against the bright flames. People were sitting on the steps of houses, and on the walls, and some called to them as they went by. One or two joined them, talking to Rye or Jobe. Azalin wondered if any of the newcomers were admiring her new clothes.

They turned a corner, and a long string of people went running past, yelling and screaming. The noise made Azalin jump, but no one else took much notice.

The new street, like the one they'd just left, was lined with small, dirty houses with fallen windowsills and cracked walls. In front of one, not far from the corner, a crowd was gathered. They were sitting on the step, on the ground in the small paved area in front of the house, and on its low, moss-grown wall. A fire was burning in the paved area, throwing orange light and stretched shadows over the bricks, reflecting in the glass left in the windows, sending showers of bright sparks and black smuts into the air.

It was to this house that they were going. Rye and Jobe stepped over the low wall, pushing aside the people seated on it. Della and Babs followed them. Sol and Dox, and Azalin and Houdin with them, went more sedately through a narrow opening in the wall.

Some of the people around the fire called out to them, and Jobe stayed to talk to someone he'd met. The rest pushed through the crowd to the door of the house, which stood open, though the entrance was blocked by people leaning against the wall or sitting on the steps. All had glasses or cups in their hands.

Some people made way for them; a man on the step obstinately stayed seated, and they all had to edge and clamber around him. He glowered unpleasantly at Azalin as she edged by, and breathed a sharp, fruity smell in her face. She gripped Dox's hand tighter.

The hall beyond was narrow and dark, and stank with a reek that made Azalin screw her face up. It wasn't any smell that she had smelt before. It was something like the smell of Dox's house, but stronger and, whatever made it, it was nasty and thick. More people were crowded in there, leaning and crouching against the walls, seated in ranks up a dark flight of stairs, all drinking, all talking. The noise of voices bouncing from the walls, of shouts, of laughter, of glasses and mugs and bottles was considerable. It racketed inside Azalin's head.

Dox dragged her through a door into yet another overcrowded, hot, reeking, noisy room. There were so many people standing that Azalin could see nothing but people's backs – she was often shoved into them. And that reek filled her nose. The noise was so great that she couldn't pick out any of the words that Dox was yelling into Rye's ear. She looked round and saw Sol standing by her. He pulled a face.

Rye and the girls struggled into the crowd and disappeared. Dox, pulling Azalin by the hand, began to elbow and shove her way out of the room again. Stumbling, Azalin followed her back into the narrow, crowded corridor and further into the house, deeper into that thick, unpleasant smell. They passed into another crammed room, and, almost immediately, to Azalin's relief, out of another door into Earth's wonderful open air again.

They were in a yard that had once been surrounded by a fence, dividing it from the yards of neighbouring houses. But this fence had been broken down, and paths led across the other yards to this one. The yard was full of people. People sat on boxes, they sat on the roof of a small outbuilding, they sat on a broken-down old sofa. They were all shouting, laughing and drinking.

"Here, here," Dox said, and sat on an upturned bucket. "You can lean on me, darling," she said to Azalin, and pulled Azalin to her. Sol sat on a brick beside Dox and Houdin, impressive in his black and white, stood beside them.

Why have we come here? Azalin wondered.

Rye, Della and Babs came to them, carrying cups, and a plate which was piled high with sandwiches. Rye gave Azalin a cup which, to her surprise, was half filled with alcohol. She didn't know what kind of alcohol – it was clear, like water – but it smelled like alcohol. She was about to say that she wasn't allowed to drink alcohol yet, but then kept quiet, and took a drink instead, out of curiosity. The drink burned her mouth, burned her throat, and was so vile that she shuddered from head to foot, and her eyes watered. Everyone around her laughed, and she was offended. They had no right to laugh at her. She gave the glass to Sol, who was nearest. "I don't want it."

They laughed again. Sol gave her a sandwich instead. She sniffed at it. The bread was white, and the meat inside thick, warm and juicy. She bit into it, and found that it was decidedly more to her taste than the drink. She hadn't realised how hungry she was.

"Non, merci," said Houdin, above her, and she looked up to see him refusing a cup of the drink that Babs was offering him.

"Bung it, ben cheat," Rye said, but Houdin shook his head.

"Don't he remind you of somebody?" Dox said, nodding towards Houdin. "He looks ever so familiar to me, but I can't place him."

"He's Rye's fetch," Della said, and looked surprised when everyone turned to her. "He bin! Rye's fetch! That's credit, Babs, innit?"

Everyone began to look from Rye to Houdin. Della took off Rye's sunglasses, and said, "Glim!"

Azalin hadn't understood Della's words, but now she understood what she meant. Rye and Houdin had the same face. It hadn't been immediately obvious, because Houdin's hair was black, and sleek; and Rye's hair stood upright stiffly and was bright yellow – and Rye's sunglasses had hidden part of his face. But now, with Rye's sunglasses removed, and looking from one face to the other, it was clear. The same hairline, the same shape of face, the same line of brows, the same shaped eyes – even though Houdin's were dark and Rye's blue. The same length and shape of nose, the same line of jaw and slope of cheekbone, the same mouth, the same chin. The same face.

While the noise of talk and laughter went on around them, everyone in their own little group fell silent. Even Azalin, who knew that Houdin wasn't what he seemed, couldn't understand it. It was eerie.

Just then Jobe rejoined them, a cup of his own in his hand. "Jobe," Sol shouted up to him, and waved a stubby little hand towards Houdin. "Crack Rye's kidder."

"Rye's kidder?" Jobe said, and then he, too, looked from Houdin to Rye. He stared.

Rye took a step nearer to Houdin. "Who you bin?"

Azalin clenched her fists, hoping that Houdin wouldn't turn himself off. He didn't. He said, "I am Houdin, named in honour of Jean Eugène Robert-Houdin, the greatest of nineteenth-century illusionists, born 1805, died 1871."

This speech created another silence. No one knew what to say.

"Can I have another sandwich?" Azalin asked. "Can I have my cup back?" She was anxious to distract people's attention. "Can I really be your maunder?"

Sol laughed. "Our maunder. Ar, we'll stall with you. What's your game?"

"Game?" Azalin asked. She looked up anxiously at Rye, who, as he slowly put his sunglasses back on, was still looking at Houdin.

"What can you do, darling?" Dox asked. "Can you dance, juggle, walk on your hands?"

"No," Azalin said, feeling rather useless. "None of those."

And then some loud strangers – strangers

to Azalin – came shoving into their little circle, slapping Rye and Jobe on the back, spilling drink, and making Della stumble and shriek. To Azalin's relief, she and Houdin were rather forgotten after that, though she did catch Rye studying them in a thoughtful way that made her feel a little uneasy.

It grew later, and darker, and noisier; and the fires blazed more fiercely in the darkness and threw up fountains of orange sparks. Azalin was very tired, and when Dox said, "Let's go back," she was glad. She and Dox, with Houdin following, struggled out of the house and back through the streets, skirting more fires. When they reached Dox's libken, Dox paused in the hall, to light candles inside jam-jars, and she lit their way to the room full of clothes and mattresses, where she lit more.

"You tired, Sweetness?" Dox said. "You just lie yourself down somewhere and have a little sleep. You want some tea? It's a bit cold."

Azalin didn't want tea. She lay down on what seemed the cleanest of the mattresses – though it didn't smell clean – closed her eyes and tried to sleep. "Here," said Dox's voice and, opening her eyes again, she saw Dox bending over her, offering her something. It was a lump of hard, sweet toffee. "Summat to go beedy-bidey with," she said. Azalin took the toffee stickily into her fist and gave it a lick or two before falling into a doze again. Dox seemed kind, even if she did treat her like a baby.

She couldn't fall asleep completely because Dox got Houdin to sit beside her on the sofa and they talked. Or, rather, Dox talked – and talked and talked – and Houdin occasionally said, "Oui, Madame," or "Non, Madame." Dox would often laugh at something she had said herself, a high squeal that always woke Azalin with a start. And then the others all came back together, and it was no use even trying to sleep. She sat up and gnawed at her toffee.

Rye and Della were holding each other and dancing, stumbling, over the mattresses, blankets and pillows. Jobe, his arm around Babs, was carrying a jug of drink, and Sol was distributing hot potatoes, urging one on Houdin, who kept politely refusing.

"Oh, me and him have had such a lovely chat!" Dox said.

"Hey," Rye said, breaking his dance with Della, and staggering across the room until he bumped into the clothes-hung wall. "Let's go your duds, ben." He pushed himself away from the wall and moved towards Houdin, who had got up from the sofa. When Houdin didn't respond, Rye took hold of the lapels of his jacket and started trying to take the jacket off.

Azalin, kneeling up on her mattress, watched and didn't know what to do. No one else was taking much notice, and Houdin made no attempt to stop Rye tugging his jacket off. Once it was off, Rye threw it down on the arm of the sofa, and took off his own leather jacket, and tugged over his head the red shirt he wore underneath. His body was thin and white, and a line of dark hair grew down the centre of his chest. He held his clothes out to Houdin and, when Houdin didn't offer to take them, he threw them on the sofa too.

"Hey, Daddy!" Rye called to Sol. "Daddy! Me and him being fetches– " he pointed to Houdin's face, so close to and so like his own "We could play a vanish!"

"A vanish!" Sol said, and appeared to think. "Ar – we could knock your block off!"

Azalin had got up from her mattress and gone over to sit beside Dox, who she felt was always on her side. "What are they talking about?" she asked.

Dox put her arms around Azalin. "No, we don't want to talk their nasty talk, do we?" she said. "Remember our little maunder can't cut Rook," she said.

Rye and Sol began trying to explain what

they meant, while the others loafed on the mattresses, drank from the jug and listened. As far as Azalin could tell, they had been talking about a trick they could do, which involved making Rye appear to vanish, or which would make it seem that Rye's head had been cut off, or, possibly, both. To do the trick you needed two people who looked like each other.

"You can make them look like each other by dressing them the same and painting their faces like clowns," Dox translated, after Rye and Sol had gabbled excitedly at some length. "But with Rye and Houdin looking like twins anyway, you wouldn't have to. It'd work beautiful."

"Next door to credit!" Rye said and, feeling that the explanations were over, he turned to Houdin again, and began to unbutton Houdin's shirt. A real person would have stopped him, but Houdin just stood there. It was up to Azalin.

She stood up and demanded, "What are you doing?"

Everyone looked at her in surprise. Dox offered her another piece of toffee.

"I'm dudding up in his togs," Rye said. "Glim how I glaz."

"Leave him alone!" Azalin said. But they only laughed, and Rye undid the last few buttons of the shirt. Pulling it open, he stopped. Then he dropped the edges of the shirt and stepped back. He turned a puzzled face to Sol, who got up from the mattress he was sitting on and went over to stand beside Rye. Jobe and Babs got up and went to stand behind them.

Feeling unhappy, Azalin moved to where she could see what they were all looking at. Dox came with her.

No time had been wasted on the parts of Houdin that were meant to be covered by clothes. His chest was smooth and featureless, except for the faintly outlined hatch just underneath where his ribs should have been.

Sol took hold of Houdin's shirt cuff and tugged until the whole sleeve slid from Houdin's shoulder and down his arm. Rye took the other sleeve and, between them, they pulled the shirt off. Other panels were revealed in Houdin's arms.

Everyone turned and looked at Azalin.

•NINE•

Deborah, Vashti and Hassan were sitting on the soft chairs of the Committee room's waiting area. Tired, they sprawled, with heads propped on hands, or resting against cushioned arms.

Gina, coming to find them, said, "There's news."

They stirred, opened eyes, sat up. They had been waiting for hours. "What?" Hassan asked.

"It's not all good, I'm afraid," Gina said. "I think it's better if you come to the office."

Mary Mboko was in her office and looked up without smiling as they entered. "Oh, Gina found you. Please sit down," she said. "I've just heard that the Earth Police have found some sightings of Azalin. They have moved with exemplary speed." Her tone suggested, Deborah thought, that the Earth authorities were being far more helpful than such unsporting people deserved.

"Is Azalin safe?" Hassan asked. Deborah kept her arms folded and her mouth closed, and waited for the worst.

"She was alive and safe when last sighted." Miss Mboko was looking at a small computer screen on her desk, and she frowned. "It's difficult to understand Earthtime . . . However, what matters is that Azalin was seen getting out of a – a luggage compartment of a vehicle, a passenger vehicle. She had, evidently, smuggled herself into the compartment." Again, Miss Mboko's tone was disapproving.

"She was a long way from where she started – not even in the same country. That's why the Police couldn't find any trace of her before." Miss Mboko gave Deborah the merest glance from the corner of her eye, but her meaning was clear. "If you hadn't been so unsporting as to keep back the message from your unsporting daughter, we wouldn't have had all this trouble looking for her."

Gina, trying to lighten the rather heavy atmosphere, said, "But she's been sighted since then."

Miss Mboko raised her voice very slightly, firmly silencing Gina. "Azalin had managed to get herself carried to a theme park. Do you know what that is? A recreational area, apparently enclosed. That's where she phoned you from, Miss Rupkina."

She paused, and looked sternly at Deborah, who wanted to tell her to get on with what she had to say. But, conscious that she had been stupid and unsporting, Deborah lowered her head and looked away instead.

"It seems that in this theme park they have some enormously expensive and sophisticated robots – and it seems that Azalin has stolen one."

"What?" Hassan said. "My daughter's not a thief!"

"Forgive me for speaking plainly, Mr Fairman. These robots, I'm told, sometimes malfunction, switch themselves on and have been known to walk a little way by themselves – but never far. The technicians at the theme park feel that this one only walked so far because Azalin was with it. They think that she stole it.

Before Hassan could say anything else, Deborah broke in. "The last sightings of my daughter?" She was still standing with her arms folded.

"Azalin was seen leaving the theme park with the robot, and she was also seen later, er– " Miss Mboko broke off, in a way that made Deborah suddenly uneasy. "I hate to have to give you news like this . . . On Earth they have people with no jobs, no trade, who perform in public places, hoping that people will give them money. They are often thieves too . . ." She spoke with distaste. "Azalin was seen with some of these people."

Hassan and Deborah and Vashti looked at each other in shock.

"What's more, she was seen walking with these people into what they call on Earth `a no-go area'."

"And that means?" Hassan demanded.

"Very much what it says. These are places, apparently, where thieves and unsporting people live – people so unsporting that not even the Earth authorities risk going there." She looked at their horrified, frightened faces and said, "Oh, Hassan, Deborah, I'm so sorry. Vashti, I'm sorry. There is hope, you know, there is hope."

Deborah had sat heavily on a chair, and had slumped forward. Miss Mboko got up from her own chair and bent over her.

"I asked what was going to be done, and I've been assured – assured, Deborah, that the authorities are going to find Azalin and bring her out of there."

"How?" Deborah asked. "If they can't go there themselves?"

"They are going to send in troops," Miss Mboko said. "Armed men. They're going to find Azalin and bring her out safely, don't worry."

Miss Mboko had talked for a long time with an officer of the Earth Police Force which was presently looking for Azalin, but she didn't feel it was the right time to tell Azalin's parents everything that the Earther woman had said: "I'll be blunt, Miss Mboko: they might get the little girl out of there, and I hope they do, but they're going in after the robot. Because it's worth so much, and the theme park's making a row about it. And to clean out the no-go. They're getting too cheeky in there."

Deborah began to cry, with strange whinings, snufflings, gulps. "It's my fault. If I hadn't – if I'd told sooner – my fault."

Vashti put her arms around her sister, but the others stood and watched her cry.

"Well, she might have been found sooner if you'd told us about the message sooner," Miss Mboko said, ignoring an angry glare from Vashti. "But we can't know that for sure."

"What if she's killed?" Deborah cried. "What if she's killed?"

•TEN•

"A goid," Rye said.

Everyone was looking at Azalin. Sol said, "Bin you a goid an' all?"

"No," Dox said. "No, Sol. I saw her undress, remember? Her's no goid."

They had all backed off from Houdin, as if he was somehow dangerous. Azalin went to stand by the robot.

"If her's no goid–" Rye said.

Sol finished for him. "Then how did you strike it?"

Azalin held Houdin's hand in its now rather grubby white glove. It made her feel a little better. "I didn't strike him," she said. "He was running away by himself. I went with him, that's all."

"If I had stayed," Houdin said, "I would have been reprogrammed."

They all stared at Houdin again. Some even edged a little further away. "It cuts," Rye said.

"It always did," Azalin pointed out.

"But I didn't know it was a goid . . ."

Babs looked over Rye's shoulder. "How come it's got your fizzog, Rye?"

"Ar!" Rye was suddenly angry. "He ain't my fetch – it was made to look like me! Daddy, how come? How come it's got my fizzog?"

Sol shrugged. "Ask it."

Rye stepped close to Houdin. "How come you look like me? How come you got my face?" He gave the robot a push, and Azalin heard the whirr as Houdin turned himself off. Rye, angry, threw Houdin down on the mattresses.

"Don't!" Azalin said.

"You," Sol said to her, "got some questions to answer. Where'd you come from? We know where that come from." He pointed to Houdin. "Only one place that could come from — the Punter Prison. But where'd you come from?"

Azalin guessed that the Punter Prison must be the theme park. "I come from the Punter Prison too."

"What? You moil there? Work, I mean, work."

Azalin wondered whether to say yes, but couldn't figure out what trouble the lie might get her into. "No . . ." she said uncertainly.

"You come from the Punter Prison, but you don't work there?"

Rye was crouched over Houdin, pulling off the rest of the robot's clothes. "But Sol, why's it got my fizzog?"

"Rye, will you zip—?"

"Hey, Rye," Della said. "Mind that time them ruffs was clicking you?"

"Hey, ar!" Babs said. "Mind?" She mimed the action of taking a photograph. "Clicking and clicking they was, mind – you and Sol was showing out, and they was clicking."

"Lots of ruffs click we when we show out," Rye said.

"All light?" Della asked. "These clicked all light."

Rye looked thoughtful. "I mind . . ."

"They was scribbling an' all," Babs said, and pretended to write in the air.

"They struck me fizzog!" Rye said, and he drew back his foot and kicked Houdin hard.

"Don't!" Azalin said. She crouched down beside Houdin, but couldn't stop Rye kicking the robot again. "Sol, make him stop!"

"Rye– " Sol began.

"A goid!" Rye said. "And they give it my fizzog! My shows! It took me donkeys to get them shows! I got banged up, I hurt. It does 'em by electric, and with my fizzog!"

"Rye," Sol said.

"They won't let me in the punters, they won't gelt me to show-out to the punters – ah, no, I'm Rookery trash! But they strike my fizzog and my shows and give `em to a goid!"

"Rye, zip up," Sol said. "Don't your cap ever buzz? You see this goid? You think they gifted we with it?"

Rye did shut up then, and looked at Jobe, who was standing with his arms folded.

Sol turned back to Azalin. "I'll try and mind to talk your whidder," he said. "If you come from the Punter Prison and you don't work there . . . You didn't gelt, I mean, pay, to get in, did you?"

"No," Azalin said. Since Houdin was no protection or comfort, she had gone to Dox, and was sitting beside her on the sofa.

"How did you get in there, then, Sweetheart?" Dox asked.

Azalin looked up at her. "A coach." She decided that she'd better tell the whole truth. "You know the place where they put the bags? I got in there. When I got out I was in the Prison."

Dox and Sol exchanged a look. From her pocket Dox took a bright red sweet and pressed it into Azalin's hand. "And how did you get the goid, my love?" Dox asked.

"I told you. I didn't. He was already walking around by himself when I found him.

He wanted to get out of the – the park, so I just went with him."

"It's a goid," Rye said. "How can it truck by itself? Her's slantin."

"He's coming alive," Azalin said. "Goids do. They learn things . . ." She didn't know how to explain.

Sol said, slowly and carefully, "Where did you come from afore you got into the coach?"

"Tell we, Sweetness," Dox said, putting an arm around her.

"I don't know," Azalin said.

"You don't know?"

"I mean, I don't know where on Earth I was . . ." Azalin tried to remember, but she'd heard many names while she'd been on Earth, and none of them had meant anything much to her. "Before I came to Earth, I came from Newarth," she said.

They stared at her again. Rye and Della, Babs and Jobe drew closer, and they all stared at her.

"From Newarth?" Dox said eventually. "Sol, ain't that– ?"

"The outer-space place," he said. "You come from – up there?" Azalin nodded. "How? How did you get down here?"

"I came with a class trip, with my schoolteacher. Miss Ateba. I bet she's mad. I ran away."

"School," Sol repeated. "Schoolteacher?"

Della leaned forward. "Can you read?"

"Yes," Azalin said. Della straightened up, impressed, and looked around at the others.

"And write?" Babs asked.

"Yes."

They all looked at her in silence. Babs leaned forward and almost whispered, "Have you got a mother?"

"Everybody's got a mother," Azalin said.

Babs and Della looked at each other. "And a dad?" Della asked.

"Yes!" Azalin said.

Babs and Della and Rye and Jobe all looked at each other, and then they turned to stare at her again. Azalin felt that they thought her even stranger than Houdin. In the silence, a sound from outside became heard: a faint, distant ringing, a repeated banging. Azalin saw Rye and Jobe hear it, and turn towards it.

Sol said, "Folks, we got pain."

Rye and Jobe stopped listening to the sounds from outside and turned back to Sol. Everyone was giving him their attention.

Sol pointed from Azalin to Houdin. "The busies am going to come hungry for a slice of Rook pie."

"You reckon?" Rye said.

"Do I reckon?" Sol pointed again at Houdin. "The whole Thatching Rookery turned to gold ain't the price of that."

Rye and Jobe looked at one another again. "Hark," Jobe said. The sound from outside of banging and ringing was a little louder. Jobe turned and went into the hall, Rye following. The others stood in silence, waiting for them to come back, and listening. There were other sounds, besides the banging: a long, quivering howl rose up and fell away; a sudden, sharp, staccato drumming on something hollow and metallic. They sounded sinister, as they drifted lazily and faintly through the darkness, over the roofs of the Rookery.

Rye and Jobe came back quicker than they'd gone, rattling down the passage, falling in through the door.

"It's the call!" Jobe said.

"Wagons, biters, busies," Rye said. "Guns, cannon – they'm ringing the Rook, they'm coming in." They must have left the door at the end of the passage open, and the noises from outside seemed louder and more real: sounds like big saucepan lids being banged on tiled walls, like huge spoons being beaten on pans. Azalin edged closer to Dox, and Dox's arm tightened around her.

"We gotta shog, Sol," Rye said, and Jobe nodded.

"Hang on," Sol said.

"We gotta shog – they'm coming to eat

Rook pie, we gotta give 'em a taste!"

"We'll shog an' all," Della said. "We can chuck bibbles."

"Nobody shog!" Sol said. It was surprising that such a big voice could come from such a little body. Everyone became quiet. "Odds on," Sol said, "they'm touring for the wind-up toy and the kinchmo. What goes down, bennies, if they catch we with 'em?"

Jobe laughed, a noise louder even than the whistles, bangs and howls from outside. "They'll measure we wazzins for a rope collar."

Sol nodded. "We'll do the midair shuffle."

Rye's hand went to his throat.

"So," Sol said, and pointed at Azalin and Houdin, "when the busies come in, they'd better not be here."

Everyone was staring at Azalin again. She was beginning to find being stared at worrying.

"So," Sol said, "what we going to do with 'em?"

Outside, in the dark, the call went on and on: bangs, clangs, whistles, howls, shouts. Inside, everyone still stared at Azalin.

•ELEVEN•

Azalin felt scared. These people, who'd seemed friendly enough, didn't seem friendly any more. Even Dox had moved a little away from her and was staring at her as if she didn't know her. And there lay Houdin on the mattresses, stripped, and switched off. Useless, cowardly robot. Why did she always have to cope on her own? She was beginning to be tired of it.

"You don't have to do anything with us," she said to Sol, trying to sound brave and calm. "Just let us go."

Sol laughed. He sat down on the mattresses as a child sits, his short legs stuck out in front of him. Azalin glanced round at the others. Jobe was staring down at her through his beard and hair, his arms folded. Della stood legs astride, with her hands on her hips. Rye was holding his own shoulders and glowering. Dox seemed upset.

"How can we let you go?" Sol asked. "You

know what's going down out there? You lug the call?"

She could. The noise outside – the call – was getting louder all the time, and closer: a steady metallic banging, high-pitched ululating squeals and whistles. She shivered, listening to it. "Rookery war," Sol said. "That means the busies am coming in."

"We should shog, Dad," Rye said.

"Zip it," Sol said. To Azalin, he said, "The busies am come touring for you and for that." He pointed to Houdin. "But they ain't going to ask nicely where you bin. They'm going to fire libkens, they'm going to box folk. In your whidder, that means kill people."

Azalin felt quite giddy with fright when she heard this. The idea that, on the other side of these walls, out there where that eerie noise was being made, were people who intended to kill other people, and it was almost impossible to believe, and yet she was being told it was the truth. "No," she said. It came out in a whisper and no one heard.

Rye said, "We'll rip 'em."

Sol laughed again. "He's going to try," he said to Azalin. "Our lads'll try to rip 'em– "

"And we," Della said.

"They'll rip we, more like," Sol said. "We ain't got armoured cars and cannon. Where you going to go if we let you go, littl'un? You think you're going to find many friends out there, when you've brought the busies in?"

Azalin tried to speak, and found that her voice was gone. That rising, falling, clamorous noise was still going on outside, and it was making Jobe and Rye edgy. They kept turning towards the door, and pacing in little circles, eager to answer the call. She really didn't want to go outside, but she didn't want to stay here and find out what they were going to do with her and Houdin either. She coughed, and managed to say, "Nobody would know it was me the busies wanted."

Sol looked at her pityingly. "Just 'cos we didn't know who you were, don't mean nobody else does," he said. "And everybody in the Rook knows everybody else. One glaz and they'd pin you for an outie. When a Rookery war starts, darling, no outies are welcome in the Rook. So what are we going to do with you?"

Rye moved so suddenly and so fast that Azalin thought he was going to hit or kick her. He swooped down over her and she flinched back, but it was Houdin he was after. He lifted the robot up and dropped it beside Sol. "Brog it," he said. "Dosh its bits."

It wasn't hard to guess that he meant to break Houdin into pieces. "You can't!" Azalin said.

Rye ignored her. "Gotta be some power unit in it – dosh that. Wiring, circuitry, discs – dosh it. Brog the rest and– "

Azalin floundered over the mattresses and sheets on hands and knees, grabbed at Houdin and tried to drag him away. "You can't do that, shan't let you!"

Rye, crouching, showed his teeth at her in anger, and smacked her across the face.

"Hey!" shouted Sol and Jobe together.

Azalin drew back sharply from the blow, and rolled from her knees to her side. Her cheek was bruised against her bones, and stung, but the smack hadn't hurt much more than a knock she might have given herself. It was shock more than anything that knocked her sideways.

A shadow fell over her as the big shape of Jobe moved above her. "Felching a babby!" Jobe said, and made a swinging motion towards Rye, who went over backwards. Then Dox was picking Azalin up.

"All right, Sweetness, all right? No felching, we said," she shouted at Sol. "Nobody felches anybody this libken!"

"Her ain't this libken!" Rye said, in a sulky and oddly tearful voice, which made Azalin look at him from Dox's arms. He was sitting on the mattresses, glowering at her, and blood was running down from his nose and over his lips and chin.

"Her's a babby!" Jobe said, and made another sudden movement. Rye pushed himself further away with his feet. Then he looked at Azalin again. She could see that he blamed her for his bleeding nose.

Azalin looked round. Nobody seemed to care very much that Jobe had hit Rye. Dox was still fussing over her and asking her if she was all right. Della and Babs were standing by the door, tense, but on the sidelines. Jobe was scowling at Rye, but Rye was rather carefully not looking at Jobe – his attention was on Azalin instead, and Azalin didn't like that at all.

"Stymied?" Sol demanded. "Blagging sawnies! Babbies yourselves! We brog the gizmo then nobody'll ever know we had it. But what–?"

"No!" Azalin said.

Dox had seated herself on the mattresses, and was holding Azalin on her lap, hugging her. "Ssh," she said. "Don't argue, Sweetness. Hush up."

"But you can't!"

"Ssh!"

"What do we do with the kinchmo?" Sol asked.

From outside came a sudden increase in the noise: a rolling, dull, drumming noise, that had hardly started before it was pierced by high shrieks and yells. Everyone paused and lifted up their heads to listen.

Rye wiped the back of his hand across his face, smearing blood across his cheek. "It's going up," he said.

Sol sighed, and repeated wearily, "What do we do with the kinchmo?"

"Dosh it," Rye said, sending a hard look at Azalin.

Azalin thought she hadn't heard right. Sell her? You couldn't sell people.

No one else said anything, but all looked thoughtful. Encouraged, Rye said, "Dosh it. To Glazzer. He'll bing her north. We'll get summat out of it, and nobody'll know her was with we."

"You can't sell me," Azalin said. The idea was so strange it was almost funny, though she didn't quite feel like laughing. She looked at Jobe, who was standing above her. She twisted round to look at Dox. Neither of them said anything.

Rye grinned at her and then put his fingers quickly to his hurt face. "Or box it," he said. He looked sidelong at Sol, who didn't move or speak. "Box it," he repeated. "Chuck the quarrom over the wall to Tobby's grunters, turn it to rashers. Nobody'll know it was ever here." Again he looked sidelong at Sol.

He doesn't mean it, Azalin thought. He can't mean it. But no one else was saying anything. She wondered what it would feel like to be killed. How would they do it? I'm not scared, she told herself; but her heart was pounding.

"Sol," Dox said, "I don't like this kind of talk."

"Don't you brevit, lovely," Sol said. "It bain't Rye cuts what we do. What Rye's going to do is hike the kinchmo to the busies."

"Who? Me?" Rye demanded.

"You. Jobe'll brog the goid."

Azalin fought out of Dox's arms, threw herself on top of Houdin, and wrapped her arms round him. "No, no, no!"

Rye moved, reaching for Azalin. Jobe stepped forward – Rye drew back.

Dox bent over Azalin. "Sweetness, you've got to let go. It's OK, we're going to see you get home."

"You can't break him up," Azalin said. "He's coming to be like a person. I won't let you."

Sol edged himself alongside her. "Hark," he said. "We thought you was Rookery folk, like we. We took you in, treated you good. They snag we with you – or this thing – they'll string we up. Know what that means? Rope round we necks till we dead. That's me, Rye and Jobe, for sure. You want that?"

Azalin sat up, though she still kept a firm hold on Houdin. "Would they do that? Really?"

"Hang we?" Sol said. "Hang Rookery men? Sweetness, they'd party while we was choking. Nobody's got any use for we but we. They might not hang folk up there in Heaven, where you come from, but they do down here."

"I don't – " Azalin felt shamefully close to crying. "I don't want them to hang you." She looked at Rye. Except him, perhaps. But no – despite the slap, she really didn't want Rye to be hanged either. "They won't know," she said. "There's lots of people in the Rookery. They won't know it was you, I won't tell them. They won't be able—"

"Azalin, bab," Sol said. "They'll be looking for somebody to blame. They've sent the busies in. They'll want somebody to string up. Folk have glimmed you with we. Somebody'll tell 'em, if they gelt enough to find out.

"Well . . ." Azalin said. From outside came a boom, a cracking bang that made her flinch. But then she remembered what she'd been saying. "If you break him up and sell him, then the people you sell the parts to – they'll know you had him. They'll tell on you."

Jobe laughed and said, "Bab's got you there, Sol."

Sol smiled, but shook his head. "That's weeks to come," he said, "afore we sell the bits. Busies'll be gone and Rookery'll be ours again. Smoking, but ours. But we've got to get rid of it now. The bits, they'll be easier to hide than that big thing. If they catch us with that–"

"If," Azalin said, "if I help you break him up, can I have one bit of him?" The idea she'd had was so wonderful she could hardly get the words out.

"No!" Rye said, but Sol held up his stubby little hand.

"What bit would that be, Sweetness?"

"The hard disc." From the corner of her eye, she saw Rye move. and knew that he was going to object, so hurried on. "You couldn't sell it! It's the program that boots him up – that's all it's good for. You can't get rid of the program without ruining the disc, and it'll have the manufacturer's name all over it. If you're caught with that, they'll know you had Houdin as well. So give it to me."

Sol sat looking at her, considering. "Why do you want it?" he asked.

"The hard disc is him," she said. "It's got everything on it that makes him Houdin –

and he's my friend, so I want it. Honest, it's no use to you."

Sol, still suspicious, considered.

"Give me a screwdriver," she said. "I know something about 'tronics – robots. I'm going to be a 'tronic. I am. I can strip it down for you."

Jobe reached a big, hairy hand down over her shoulder, offering her a big screwdriver. Azalin laughed. "That's too big!" She looked at Sol. "Can I have the bit? One bit?"

Sol looked at Dox, who nodded. Sol sighed. "Anything for a quiet life. You can have it."

Outside, in the dark, the din of banging surrounded the house, punctuated by mechanical screams and firework whooshes and explosions. Inside, Azalin sat astride Houdin and studied him. Below the access hatch was a slot with a tiny button beside it.

"We should shog," Rye said. He was pacing up and down the room again. He came to a halt, his head raised, listening to the ascending scream of some missile or rocket. Della went over to him, put her arms around him, and they leaned together.

Azalin pressed the tiny button beside it and a disc flipped out into her hand.

Immediately there was a whirr, and Houdin sat up, his eyes opening, forcing her back on to his legs. Looking into his face, she felt curiously embarrassed, especially as she was holding his function disc in her hand. Quickly, she threw it to Sol. "You can sell that," she said.

Houdin began trying to get up, threatening to spill Azalin on to the floor. Babs and Jobe at once leaped forward and seized the robot by the shoulders, trying to force it back on to the mattress. But Houdin was stronger than he looked.

"Houdin! Houdin!" Azalin cried, hoping that he could pick her words out of all the other noise. "I'm going to take out your hard disc! I'm going to keep it – I am. They'll break up the rest of you, but I'll have your hard disc, I'll have your hard disc."

Houdin stopped struggling and sat still. Jobe and Babs stood poised by him, ready to struggle with him again. Azalin looked up at Jobe. "Have you got a screwdriver small enough for these screws?"

Jobe nodded, and said to Della, who was nearest the door, "Box at end of hall."

Della let go of Rye, went out and came back with several screwdrivers. She held them out to Azalin, offering her a choice. Azalin chose the best one, and began undoing the screws that fastened down the hatch in Houdin's chest.

Houdin sat quite still, staring out over her

head, rather like a human being having some unpleasant operation, such as an injection, performed on them. Azalin took the hatch right off and threw it aside. Behind it, in the shadowed hollow of Houdin's body, were circuit boards and wires. The hard disc was in there somewhere, too. It had to be. Azalin wanted to remove the hard disc first, before she got tired and lost concentration – because it was the hard disc that would contain Houdin. All the basic programming to boot him up, and anything additional that he'd self-learned. She found the disc unit and partly removed it, and asked Rye – who was nearest – to hold it while she unfastened the tiny wires. She was rather like a surgeon who asked a colleague to hold a heart while she cut through the last little veins that held it into the body. As she removed the last wires, Houdin went off. His eyes – she had to remind herself that they were only mechanical – fixed. The arm lifted slightly and locked; his head ground round a fraction of an inch and stopped. Azalin had to grit her teeth. It was like killing someone. Except that this someone could be brought back to life again. It was all on the disc. She hoped.

She turned to take the disc unit from Rye and found him staring at Houdin. His face was white and fixed with strain. It was like seeing Houdin's face again and she looked, startled, from one to the other. There had been so many other things to think about that she'd forgotten that Houdin and Rye shared the same face. For Rye, it must have been like watching himself die.

She took the disc unit from his hand, and Rye seemed to come to himself again. His hand shot out, struck Houdin in the face, and knocked the robot's shell backwards.

Hugging the disc unit to herself, Azalin said to Sol, "This is the only bit I want."

Rye said, "That glims come a heap of dosh, Daddy."

Sol nodded towards Azalin. "The bab gets it."

Rye looked sulky. Azalin made to put the disc into her breast pocket, having forgotten that she wasn't wearing her Newarth overalls any more. For a moment she didn't know what to do: then she just stuffed the disc unit into her shirt. Her belt stopped it from falling out at the bottom. It was a scratchy, uncomfortable thing to carry around in such a way, but it was the best she could do.

"Schnell!" Rye said. He was half pacing, half dancing about the room, listening to the noise from outside. He paused for a moment, and everyone else looked up at a wave of screeching and yelling that seemed just the other side of their walls, very close.

Azalin, screwdriver in hand, turned back to Houdin. "I'll take the power unit out for–"

Jobe's hand came from behind her and took the screwdriver from her. "Shog, bab."

A little bewildered, Azalin looked round.

"Oh, Sweetness!" Dox said, and hugged her, and kissed her, very warm and soft and powdery and smelling too sweet. Azalin wriggled out of her clutch.

"Rye," Sol said. "You take her."

Rye looked round wildly. "Where?"

"Lug!" Sol said. "To the busies!"

Rye and Azalin looked at each other. "I'm not going with him!" Azalin said.

"Bennyship, shog yourself," Rye said.

"Sweetness," Sol said, "he ain't going to hurt you. But if you'm going, you'd better go now."

"I'll come," Della said.

And Azalin was hustled out into the hallway, where the bangs and shrieks and heart-jumping crashes seemed almost in her ears.

Rye was right behind her, pushing her out through a door into the cold night air that screamed and flashed.

•TWELVE•

There was a street behind them, on the other side of the house, and a street below them. From both came shouts, long howls, muffled by the damp air. Rapid rattles of running feet, and laughter. Repeated banging, thumping blows and drummings. Beams of white light shot into the air, lighting a wall, veering over the sky, then vanishing.

A crumping bang, louder than the others, came from below them, and made them all flinch. They looked towards the sound, and saw more flashes of glaring white light. A bubble and babble of shrieks rose from the same place.

In the dim light, Azalin saw Della and Rye look at each other. "La," Rye said, nodding towards the light and noise. Della took Azalin's hand, and they started across the yard.

Azalin tripped several times. The yard was full of rubbish, some of it metal and hard on the shins. It wasn't easy to cross in the half-darkness. At the end of the yard was a dying hawthorn hedge, more gaps than hedge. They passed between two dark thickets of hawthorn. On the other side, dimly seen, was a brick wall, and from behind it came an animal smell, and a restless thumping, a kicking, and a shrill squealing, like metal being scraped on metal. Whatever was behind there was disturbed by all the noise. Rye stopped by the wall for a moment.

"Tobby's grunters," Rye said. "Help me chuck her in, Dell."

"Leave it," Dell said, and pushed past him.

They started down the steep slope into the back yards of the street below. As they were nearing the walls of the houses, Azalin heard another sound – a rattling, roaring sound that came from the air above. "Deck!" Rye said, and lay down on the ground. Della and Azalin lay beside him. Azalin tried not even to breathe too deeply, in case the movement made her noticeable.

The din got louder, shuddering the air, deafening them to all other sound. Azalin didn't dare to try to look up to see what the noise was. Just when she thought her head would burst from the racket, it seemed to lessen suddenly, and then lessened more, and faded rapidly.

Della tapped Azalin's back and, slowly, carefully, Azalin sat up. Rye was already crouching, and he pointed at a black shape moving away through the sky, just above the rooftops. A beam of light suddenly shone downwards from it.

"Shog!" Rye said, and they scuttled from where they were, and around the side of the house, but stopped at the house corner, crouching down in the shelter of a low wall, and an old door which was propped on its side. From there, they could see a little of the street.

Small scattered fires were burning, handfuls of scattered flame. A smell wafted to them of burning, of smoke. Then a stammer of running feet and into view came a running crowd, shouting, leaping as they raised arms and threw. A second later, and they heard the clangs, ringing clangs as the bricks struck, bangs, clatters. And then people were running back into view, as if running away, only to turn and run forward again.

Azalin wished she was somewhere else. She didn't like this at all. She didn't like Rye crawling forward to peer around the edge of the old door. His head would get hit by a big stone. She expected stones to come over the edge of the door and fall on them. The shouts and screams made her shiver, and then go on shuddering. There was a wildness, a terror about those noises in the darkness.

"Shog!" Rye said, and from a crouch he rose and went running away up the street, in the opposite direction to the way the stones were being thrown. Della ran after him, pulling Azalin after her by the hand. Azalin looked back as they ran, and saw stones falling and clanging on upheld shields.

Rye ran across what had once been a front garden, leaped from a low wall into the street, and ran across the street behind the jagged, advancing and retreating line of stone-throwers. Della and Azalin caught him up on the other side of the street, as he jumped over a wall and ran up an entry beside another house. He stopped, leaning against the house wall, and they leaned beside him.

The noise ahead of them was worse than behind them. Din of engines, shouts, bangs, smashing of things breaking. Bright lights flashed and flickered across the entry's opening and on its walls. Azalin suspected something that she didn't really want to think about, but when she saw Rye edging along the wall towards the flashing lights and the noise, she tugged at Della's sleeve and said, "We're going towards it!"

"What?"

"We're going towards the fighting!" Della

just stared at her, the edge of her face brilliantly illuminated for one second, and then flicking into darkness. "We should be going away from it!" Azalin said. She felt herself shaking again, shaking in her shoes, bumping herself against the wall. She didn't want to go anywhere near those flying stones and that smashing glass. She could imagine a stone hitting her.

Della edged along the wall after Rye, and tried to pull Azalin after her. Azalin held back. "Hark," Della whispered. "These guards'll have summat else to think about beside we. We can slip by them. Come on."

Azalin still didn't want to go, but she allowed Della to drag her along the entry to the other end, where Rye was crouching, peering out on to the street. She flinched back, hiding behind Della, as a vast grinding roaring vehicle went past, blazing light in front of it and sideways, at them. Reverberating sounds of things hitting its sides followed, and angry shouts, and a loud, cracking, whacking sound that made her ears thrum and was – was it? She couldn't believe it – was it gunfire? She'd heard gunfire on disc-shows, a few times, but this was louder, far louder, and far more frightening. It shook the air, it hurt her ears, and made her heart hammer.

"Shog," Rye said, almost in a whisper, and started forward.

Azalin started back. "No!"

Rye, crouching, turned on one heel to look back. "Eh?"

"We'll get shot, we'll get shot if we go out there!"

Rye reached back and got hold of both her wrists. He was stronger than Della and dragged her forward, scraping her knees and shoes over the ground. She tried to wriggle back down the entry, but he got his arm round her and held her tight. When he spoke, she could feel his breath on her hair and face. "Harken," he said. "See the vans? That's where the busies be, turning ken to ken. Past them, that's where the gaffers'll be, cosy. We'll get you to the gaffers."

Azalin didn't know what he meant, and she still didn't want to go, but she was too confused and too scared to argue. She didn't want to go out there, but she didn't want to stay where she was either. She wanted to be anywhere else – even Newarth. Even doing a storekeeper's job.

Rye got up and walked out into the street, moving quickly, holding Azalin close to him and pulling her along. Della came close behind. To their right the street was quiet and empty, except for the massive shape of a van –

but it was shining its light away from them. To their left was a great deal of frightening noise. The busies were going into a house and, from the banging, the screeches, the crashes, seemed to be breaking everything in it. Things – flying too fast to be recognised – were being thrown from the doorway. On the road outside was another massive van, shining its white light on the house. Rye and Della were walking towards the van and, what was worse, they were taking Azalin with them. She could hardly breathe. She was staring at the van. In the top of it stood busies, with rifles. Great masks, or helmets, covered their heads. They're going to kill us, Azalin thought, they're going to shoot us. There would be one of those great loud deafening bangs, and a bullet would tear into them.

She knew it was going to happen – a busy saw them. She saw the blank of his helmet turn towards them. She knew it was going to happen and it was happening. The busy raised his rifle and pointed it at them. She knew it was going to happen; they were going to get shot.

"Stop!" the soldier yelled, and his rifle was pointing at them. "Stand still!" Three busies were pointing rifles at them. They were going to be shot. A bullet was going to tear through her. She'd known it was going to happen, and it was happening . . .

Rye and Della stopped, and stood looking up at the rifles and the busies holding them. Azalin leaned hard against Rye's side, trembling and trembling. The soldiers just stood there, on top of the van, glaring at them with those blank helmets, pointing the rifles.

"We're trying to get home!" Della called out, and her voice cracked and screeched with fright. She put her arms around Rye, holding his arms to his side. "We've got nothing to do with this – look, we've got the babby with we! We'm just trying to get home. Please – we'm just trying to get home!"

Still the busies stood up there, in the darkness flashed through with brilliant light, and noisy with bangs and shrieks. Blank, watchful helmets, and pointing rifles. They will shoot us, they will, Azalin thought. But then one jerked his helmet sideways, in the direction they were going, and lowered his rifle slightly. Della darted forward, pulling Rye and Azalin after her. They ran past the van. Azalin ran, feeling her heart pounding in every part of her body – it even seemed to pound in her feet as they struck the pavement. It was a painful, sick and terrible feeling; and every moment she thought she would hear that great loud earbashing crack of a rifle fired, and feel the bullet smack into her back.

The street beyond the van was full of clothes and bedding, broken vases, chairs – all things thrown from the houses – but was quiet. To either side stood more soldiers, holding rifles, who turned their blank helmets towards them, but didn't challenge them. They'd seen the busies on the van let them go past.

Rye pulled Della to a halt, and they went on slowly. "Bennyship, Dell," he whispered to her. "Bennyship."

To their left were two burned-out houses, burned out and ruined a long time ago. The road made a bend just by them and, just beyond the bend, joined another street. At the place where the two streets joined, vans and cars were gathered, completely blocking the way. Lights flashed on top of the cars. Busies stood around, and walked about.

Rye stopped, and crouched, pulling Azalin to him. "There's the gaffers," he said. "Dooze, dooze – fambles up – cut 'em your monick."

Azalin tried to swallow and couldn't. " I don't want to go on my own," she said. They'd shoot her, she knew they'd shoot her.